PUFFIN BOOKS

PIGGIES

Nick Gifford says:

'After years of writing for an adult audience, a friend persuaded me to aim for a different age group – I had a go and found that I loved it! I've never had so much fun writing. *Piggies* probably shows what a dark sense of fun I have . . .'

Piggies is Nick Gifford's first novel for young adults, although he has short stories published in a number of anthologies. He has also written adult novels under the name Keith Brooke. As well as writing, Nick develops web sites and lives with his wife and children in north-east Essex.

www.nickgifford.co.uk

PUFFIN BOOKS

Published by the Penguin Group
Penguin Books Ltd, 80 Strand, London WC2R 0RL, England
Penguin Putnam Inc., 375 Hudson Street, New York, New York 10014, USA
Penguin Books Australia Ltd, 250 Camberwell Road, Camberwell, Victoria 3124, Australia
Penguin Books Canada Ltd, 10 Alcorn Avenue, Toronto, Ontario, Canada M4V 3B2
Penguin Books India (P) Ltd, 11 Community Centre, Panchsheel Park, New Delhi – 110 017, India
Penguin Books (NZ) Ltd, Cnr Rosedale and Airborne Roads, Albany, Auckland, New Zealand
Penguin Books (South Africa) (Pty) Ltd, 24 Sturdee Avenue, Rosebank 2196, South Africa

Penguin Books Ltd, Registered Offices: 80 Strand, London WC2R 0RL, England

www.penguin.com

First published 2003
1

Copyright © Nick Gifford, 2003
All rights reserved

The moral right of the author has been asserted

Set in Linotype Sabon
Typeset by Rowland Phototypesetting Ltd, Bury St Edmunds, Suffolk
Made and printed in England by Clays Ltd, St Ives plc

British Library Cataloguing in Publication Data
A CIP catalogue record for this book is available from the British Library

ISBN 0–141–31489–3

21970

Contents

Change

At some point during Ben Aynsley's walk home, the world changed around him.

He didn't realize it was happening at the time, of course. It was only when he reached town that he began to spot the differences, the changes.

It was only when he reached town that his problems really began . . .

He'd been over at Andy's house in the small village of Weeley, watching football on satellite TV. After the match, they'd had a kick-about in Andy's back yard and then, with the storm clouds heaped up on the horizon, Ben had headed for home across the wasteland known as Barlow's Patch.

The storm was like no storm he'd ever experienced.

Within minutes of Ben setting out, the clouds had tumbled across the sky, blotting out the afternoon sun. As he cut across the old quarry track, the first heavy raindrops began to fall.

Ben was only wearing a light coat, so he took shelter in one of the ruined quarry buildings – a brick shell with empty window frames and a half-collapsed, corrugated tin roof.

Outside, everything was grey, the clouds overhead so dark it was like a night sky. Lightning strobed, edging the clouds with white. Rain hammered on what remained of the tin roof, and Ben backed away into its shelter.

At one point, he looked up at the dark, twisting clouds, and that must have been when it happened.

When everything changed.

The sky flickered and then the clouds seemed to bulge with light. A fork of lightning ripped across the grey and, for an instant, it was as if the sky itself was being torn apart. Ben felt a tingle of static electricity across his skin. Heart racing, he wondered if he had been struck by lightning.

Suddenly he felt powerful forces tugging at his limbs – like strong hands trying to tear him apart. He twisted, fighting the pressure; it was as though he had been pulled off the ground and was spinning in mid-air.

A heavy impact knocked the air from his lungs and he found himself flat on the ground, face in the mud.

He rose to his knees, gasping for breath. He felt sick and dizzy, his head still spinning. Where . . . ? He couldn't think straight.

He looked around. The old building was no longer there. Hadn't he been sheltering from the storm in the ruins of a quarry building?

He wiped his face with his cuff, then stood unsteadily and brushed the dust from his clothes.

Dust.

The ground was dry.

Hadn't there been a storm?

He heard voices coming from the quarry – men, shouting, arguing. That wasn't right either. The quarry had been closed for five or six years. It was surrounded with chain-link fence and barbed wire to keep children and dogs away from the old workings. There were tunnels and deep pits in there and it was easy to get lost – or so people said. You could lose yourself in there and never be found, they said, and so people tended to stay away from the place.

Paths popular with dog walkers and mountain bikers went past the quarry though. Maybe that explained the voices he could hear.

They were louder now, and definitely angry. They were arguing – the words were hard to make out, but the violent tone was unmistakable.

Ben was still shaken by the storm. He didn't know what was going on, but he knew for certain that he didn't want to meet the owners of these angry voices while he was in such a confused state. He hurried back on to the track across Barlow's Patch and soon the quarry was far behind.

He must have taken the wrong turning. That would explain it. That would explain why the allotments weren't there any more, and why the new houses on Campernell Close had been replaced by a small industrial estate – a tyre and exhaust centre, a printing company, a builders' merchants, a lorry depot.

There were dozens of paths across Barlow's Patch. They twisted and turned and crossed each other repeatedly. It was difficult to tell one area of scrubby grassland from another. That must explain it – in his confused state, Ben had followed the wrong track.

He came to the road that ran along the edge of the Patch. He crossed it and soon he came to Regent Road, just where he had expected. Ben looked along at the industrial units, puzzled. He shrugged and headed down Regent Road, past lines of bungalows that were somehow familiar and strange at the same time.

He couldn't work it out. He didn't doubt that this was Kirby. Where else could it be? He'd lived in this small town for six years, since he and his parents had moved down from Norfolk. If you head across Barlow's Patch from Weeley, the first place you reach is Kirby. Maybe that lightning had actually struck Ben – maybe it had rewired the memories in his brain, making the familiar look strange. Maybe that was why something as simple as walking home left him feeling so confused.

He came to the end of the road, where it met the main road into town. According to the sign, this wasn't Regent Road at all, but Regency Road.

Familiar yet strange.

Ben shook himself, as if that would somehow clear his mind. He followed the alleyway that formed a short cut through to the old market square in the town centre.

An elderly lady was coming the other way, a small white terrier straining at the lead. As they passed in the alley, the dog started jumping up and yapping. The woman glared at Ben as if it was somehow his fault, then pulled her dog away.

The market square was all wrong.

The shops were the same as Ben remembered – the chemist, the grocer's, the newsagent's and two estate agents. But . . . the grass and trees, the walled pond with the spitting fish fountain, were missing. In their place was a chained-off square with parking spaces painted on to it, some litter bins and some kind of display board showing a tourist map of the town.

Ben leaned against the high brick wall at the end of the alley. He pressed his forehead against the cool bricks, trying to stop his head from spinning, trying to make sense of something that quite clearly made no sense whatsoever.

Somewhere on his way back to town the world had changed. Or something in Ben's head had changed. He wasn't sure which alternative he preferred.

Love Bites

The map. The map would explain everything, Ben felt sure of that. All he had to do was pull himself together and go to look at the map.

He pushed himself away from the wall, waited for a car to pass, then headed across the main street. A few cars were parked in the spaces painted on to the square. They looked like normal cars, but the makers' badges were unfamiliar and Ben didn't recognize them. Not a Ford or a Nissan in sight.

He approached the display board. The map had been put there for holidaymakers – made to look as if it had been painted by hand, with little pictures of some of the buildings and tiny black footprints picking out interesting walks. 'The

Historical Market Town of Kirby' it proclaimed in big letters. The layout of the streets looked familiar to Ben, but some of the street names were slightly different – as he had already seen, Regent Road was now Regency Road, but also Mill Street had become Miller's Row, Hearst Green was Hart's Green, Lime Street was Lyme's Street . . . And Duke Street! According to this map, Duke Street, where Ben had lived with his parents for six years, was now called Tanner's Cut . . .

Ben heard voices. He dragged his gaze from the map. Three teenagers, about Ben's age, came running out of the newsagent's, laughing and shouting. They sprinted round the corner into . . . was it still Richard Street?

A middle-aged woman in an old-fashioned shopkeeper's apron appeared in the shop doorway, waving a hand in the air, shouting at the youths. 'Thieving little so-and-sos!' she yelled. She didn't run after them though. They had a head start and she was too heavy to give chase anyway.

She saw Ben watching and took a step towards

him. 'You with them, are you?' she demanded. 'You keepin' watch while your mates go nicking sweets and things, are you?'

Ben backed away, shaking his head. 'No,' he said. 'I don't know them. I'm not with them. I've never seen them before.'

She took another step across the road. 'You're lying,' she screeched. 'I can tell. You're a lying little so-and-so.'

Now there were some other people in the street. They must have come out of the shops when they heard the commotion. They were all staring at Ben.

He turned and ran.

He couldn't be sure, but one of the three shoplifters had looked just like his friend Andy. It wasn't possible, he knew. He'd left Andy at his cottage a mile and a half away, on the far side of Barlow's Patch. Andy hadn't been coming into town. He must be mistaken.

But he wasn't going to hang around and try to explain all that to the angry shopkeeper and the people in the street who were all staring at Ben accusingly. How could he ever begin to explain something as strange as what was happening to him this afternoon?

He headed back along the alleyway to Regency Road, then turned right, and right again into a road he knew as Beaumont Street. Sure enough, he heard the voices again a few minutes later – the three must have stopped running when they were clear of the square, confident that the shopkeeper wouldn't give chase. They appeared at a junction a short distance ahead of Ben.

He walked faster.

Mid-brown hair down to his collar, a good head taller than his friends, a casual, rolling stride – from behind it looked just like Andy. Ben didn't recognize the other two. A boy with short, dark hair and a scuffed leather jacket. A girl with spiky blonde hair and tight jeans. She was full of energy, bouncing about, pushing and poking at her two friends, talking and laughing all the time.

When he was only a few paces behind, Ben said, 'Hey, is that you, Andy?'

The three turned as one and stared at Ben. There was something in their look that Ben didn't like, something that cut right through him. The one who looked like Andy seemed puzzled for an instant, as if he was struggling to place Ben.

'I . . . Sorry,' said Ben. 'I thought you were someone else. From behind, you looked like someone else.'

The tall boy shrugged, just like Andy, and the three of them relaxed.

'You shouldn't do that,' said the girl. 'Thought you were the filth.'

They turned to walk on and Ben fell into step with them. He felt the need to explain. 'I was at the square,' he said. 'I saw you running off and you –' he nodded at the tall boy '– looked just like a friend of mine called Andy.'

The boy shook his head. 'My name's Stu,' he said.

'But we all know him as Stacker, don't we?' chipped in the girl.

That jarred Ben – he'd been joking about that with Andy while they watched football. It was something their form teacher, Mr Marshall, had said just before the summer holidays.

'Because all he'll ever be good for is stacking shelves in a supermarket, right?' said Ben.

The girl looked at him strangely, then grinned and smacked him on the arm. 'Spot on, matey,' she said. Then she added, 'My name's Rachel and the quiet one here is Lenny. Lenny hardly says a word, cos he's got a crush on me. Haven't you, Lenny?' She leaned over and kissed him on the cheek. Lenny beamed at her, his cheeks bright red.

'My name's Ben.'

'Hello, Ben. D'you fancy me too? Stacker does – he's nearly as bad as Lenny.'

What she said was clearly true, but she fancied herself more than the other two put together. Ben didn't say so though. 'That woman from the shop thought I was with you lot,' he said instead, unable to meet the girl's steady gaze. 'I had to leg it, just like you did.'

'We were just nicking,' said Rachel. 'Something to do, you know?'

'Want some?' Stacker produced a handful of chocolate bars from his jacket pocket and tossed one to Ben. 'Hate the things, myself.'

They came to the recreation ground and went in through the steel barrier that was supposed to stop kids taking bikes and motorbikes on to the playing field. They stopped behind the old sports pavilion. Its pebble-dashed concrete walls had been sprayed with graffiti – mostly Rachel's name, picked out in jagged purple letters by her or one of her admirers.

'You from round here then?' asked Rachel, suddenly intense. 'I don't know you. You don't sound like one of us.'

A harsh rattling broke through the silence that followed her question. Lenny had produced a spray can and was shaking it loudly, getting ready to paint something new on the wall.

'I . . . just moved here,' said Ben.

Rachel relaxed. 'Thought you was one of them grammar-school snobs,' she said.

The grammar school . . . She must mean Harpers College in Colchester. Ben's parents had wanted him to go to Harpers, but he had argued with them because he wanted to go to the local community high school with his friends.

'A new boy,' said Rachel. She turned to tall

Stacker and blew him a kiss. 'New boy's got a lot to learn, hasn't he?' she said.

Ben looked from one to the other. He didn't understand what they were talking about. All of a sudden he didn't want to be there with these three. He didn't know why he'd followed them. He glanced across to where Lenny was spraying the pavilion wall. Where someone had painted 'Eddie! Eddie! Eddie!' Lenny had added 'IS A PIG'.

Ben looked back at Stacker and Rachel. They were kissing.

Rachel pulled away. 'I bet new boy hasn't even had a taste of the locals yet, has he?' She grinned at him and said, 'Is that right, Ben darling? You want a taste?'

She reached out and took his hand while he stood rooted to the spot. She moved closer and kissed him on the cheek and then on the neck. He felt her teeth on his skin. 'Fancy a love bite?' she whispered.

He backed away, feeling dizzy, feeling that she was teasing him, confusing him even more. She laughed and spun away.

Lenny had finished at the wall and now he came towards Rachel. He grinned, revealing his long white teeth.

'Lenny'll show him how to do it, won't you, darling? Come on, Lenny, give me a love bite.'

Lenny lowered his head to Rachel's neck. After a second or two, Rachel gasped and her eyes opened wide. She turned to Stacker and said, 'Come on, Stu, you too. Come here,' and pushed Lenny away.

Slowly, the leather-jacketed boy turned to look at Ben. There was blood smeared all around his mouth and a peaceful, faraway look in his eyes. At his side, Stacker stooped low over Rachel's neck, lapping at the wound.

Rachel raised a hand towards Ben. 'Come on, new boy,' she gasped. 'Come and have a taste of the locals. Kirby's purest.'

Ben turned and ran, and behind him he could hear the three of them laughing and giggling, like little children at play.

No Place Like Home

Home. Everything would be OK at home.

He just had to head back to the high street and turn left into Lime Street – Lyme's Street, past the Cottage Bakery. Then head down the narrow pavement, past the big windows and hairspray smells of Cut and Dried and turn right into Duke Street.

Home. His parents would be there. Everything would be OK then.

He reached the bakery and turned left. In Cut and Dried a woman was tipped back, with her head in a basin, having the shampoo rinsed from her hair. Ben hurried on, heading for home – he had walked this way so many times before!

Duke Street. That was where Ben lived, but there was no Duke Street in this twisted world in which he had found himself. Just as the map had shown, the road that cut between Lyme's Street and New Street was called Tanner's Cut. The houses were different too – a cramped double row of Victorian terraced houses, nothing like the modern converted shop where Ben lived.

He walked from end to end of Tanner's Cut, again and again, as if somehow it would all suddenly change back to the street he knew. People started to look at him strangely. An old woman peered out from behind a lacy curtain, eyes following him as he walked. A middle-aged man watched him from under the bonnet of a battered estate.

Everything looked so familiar, yet everything had changed. A third of the way along, number 27, his home, there should have been a large double window that had once been a shop front. The bricks should have been straight-edged and modern, where the front wall had been rebuilt when the shop was converted into a house, not rounded and age-worn.

He knocked on the door, not daring to try his key.

After a short time, the door opened and an old man peered out. Ben didn't recognize him.

'Yes?' the man said, squinting at Ben.

The door was open far enough for Ben to see some of the hallway. The wallpaper was textured with a clam-like pattern and painted a faded peach. Dozens of small photographs hung from the wall, some with extra, presumably more recent, pictures tucked into their frames. The hallway must have been like that for years . . .

Ben looked at the man again.

Just then a woman's voice came from the depths of the house. 'Is that the heater man, Tom?'

They were complete strangers. In *his* house – although it was *not* his house – waiting for someone to come and fix their heating.

'What is it?' asked the man. 'Lost your tongue?'

'I . . . I think I've come to the wrong house.' The wrong *everything*.

He backed away. Up until the door opened he had been convinced that Mum or Dad would be there and that although the house and the town had changed, his parents, at least, would be there for him.

He turned and ran, aware all the time of the eyes watching him, the people thinking, *He's not from round here. He's not one of us.*

When darkness fell, more people came on to the streets.

Ben walked aimlessly around the town, his mind numbed by the helplessness of his situation. What do you do when all that you know has suddenly become unreliable? Where do you turn? He tried to keep away from the busiest areas. He didn't want people looking at him, didn't want them to see that he was new, that he didn't fit in. And he tried desperately hard not to think about what had happened at the recreation ground. He tried not to use the V-word. Rachel, Stacker and Lenny – did they drink each other's blood because they wanted to, or was it just some kind of game they'd used to frighten the new boy?

What about all these other people in the town? Were Rachel, Stacker and Lenny the freaks or, in this strange, twisted world, was it Ben who was the freak . . . ?

He must have been in a state of delayed shock or they would never have caught him so easily.

He walked past the Stonemason's Arms on the high street. As he passed the open door, the smell of cigarettes and beer and the sound of the people inside made him feel suddenly, intensely homesick. It was late in the evening by now. His parents must be worried sick. Wherever they were.

Ben was tired and hungry and he had no idea what to do.

Just after he had passed the pub doorway, two men burst out on to the street, laughing drunkenly.

Ben started to walk faster.

'Hey, kid! What you doing out at night, eh?'

He crossed the street, but the two men followed.

'Shouldn't be out at night, kid. Never know what might happen.'

He turned down a side street and that was his mistake. As soon as they were off the high street, the two drunks grew more confident.

'Hey, kid. C'mon, kid. We're only having a bit of fun, kid.'

They were closer behind him now. Ben took a deep breath, ready to run.

A big hand landed on his shoulder and swung him round to face the two men.

They were in their twenties, with shaven heads and ripped T-shirts and jeans. The one who had a hold of Ben's shoulder had words tattooed across his forehead where his eyebrows should have been: PURE OF BLOOD. He was grinning, revealing slightly pointed canine teeth.

'C'mon,' said the man. 'Kid out on the street this late on a feast night. Looking for a bit of fun, right?'

Ben was up against the wall of a terraced house. He couldn't take his eyes off the man's teeth. 'Let me go,' he managed to gasp.

'Ooooh,' mocked the man. 'We will, we will. In a little while . . .'

Across the street there was sudden light as

curtains were pulled back from a window. A face peered out at them. Ben tried to call, but his throat was dry, blocked. All that emerged was a pathetic croak.

'C'mon.' The man changed his grip so that he had a hold of a handful of Ben's jacket at the back of his neck. 'Let's go for a walk.'

The man pushed and Ben had to walk in front of him.

In the houses they passed, all the curtains were drawn closed. Ben imagined the people inside, watching TV, reading, maybe eating a meal. Normal life was so close, and yet . . . The hand at the back of his neck drove him on.

There was a churchyard down the street. That must be where these two were taking him – away from the street lights, away from the twitching curtains.

Ben drove an elbow hard and fast into his captor's side. It was like elbowing a brick wall.

The man laughed. 'This one's got spirit, hasn't he?' he said to his friend, who was lagging a few paces behind.

Just then a car came slowly up the street,

headlights blazing. While the two men were distracted, Ben managed to duck down, pulling his arms clear of the jacket. He was free!

He started to run, as fast as he'd ever run in his life. After a few seconds he glanced back. The two men hadn't given chase. They were too drunk, Ben guessed. They were arguing now. One of them was holding Ben's jacket in the air and gesturing angrily at the other.

Ben slowed his pace a little, but kept running. He came to a junction and turned right. As he ran, he tried to work out where to go. He needed to find somewhere to hide for the night. Somewhere he could relax and try to work out what had happened to him.

He turned another corner.

'Hey!'

He stopped, ready to turn back. He'd almost run into someone.

A man. Tall, with a dark-blue uniform. A policeman.

'What's going on?' the policeman said. 'What's all the hurry?'

'I . . . There were some men. Two men. They

. . . They grabbed me, tried to take me some-where.'

'OK, OK,' said the policeman. 'Calm yourself, will you? What's your name, son?'

'Ben. Ben Aynsley.'

'Right, Ben. Where do you live? Let's get you home. I'd like a word with your parents – letting a kid your age out on a feast night. Asking for trouble. So where do you live, Ben?'

Ben stared at the policeman. 'I . . . I don't know,' he said, finally. 'I don't know *where* I live.'

The police station was in the right place; a mod-ern red-brick building across Victoria Gardens from the council offices – except they were called Beaumont Gardens now.

Sergeant Adams had led Ben through to the office behind the reception desk and now he was boiling a kettle and washing some cups.

'So,' said the Sergeant. 'Are you going to tell me what you were running from?'

Ben hadn't worked out how much he could tell the policeman, but this was safe enough, he thought. 'Two men,' he said. 'Skinheads. One

25

had a tattoo where his eyebrows should have been. It said "Pure of Blood". He grabbed me, but I managed to get away and then I ran for it. I wouldn't let them . . .'

Sergeant Adams nodded. 'I know the lad you mean,' he said. 'He's spent a few nights in this place when he's had a few beers inside him. I'll have a word with him.'

The policeman came over and placed a steaming mug and a plate of sandwiches on the table before Ben. 'I don't know what your parents are up to, letting you out tonight. Asking for trouble on a feast night.' He stopped and looked closely at Ben. 'You don't understand, do you? The first of the month – a time of celebration, but some people get carried away. Thugs like your shaven-headed friend go looking for trouble.

'Are you going to tell me what really happened, Ben Aynsley? Are you going to tell me why you're so muddled you don't even know what night it is or where you live?'

Ben dipped his head. 'I don't know,' he said, finally. 'My name's Ben Aynsley. I live at number twenty-seven Duke Street. My father is a chartered surveyor and my mother works part-time at the university. That's the truth.'

Sergeant Adams sat down opposite Ben and leaned forward, with his elbows on the table. 'You've already told me all that. But, Ben,' he said softly, 'there *is* no Duke Street. There *are* no Aynsleys in the telephone book or in any of the local records I can check from the computer. My brother works at a surveyors' firm and I've just called him – he doesn't know of anyone called Aynsley, either. You don't exist, Ben Aynsley. Now, are you going to start telling me the truth?'

Ben managed to eavesdrop on part of the telephone conversation.

'. . . no name, no records . . . doesn't exist.'

'If he's a liar, he's a good one. I tell you, he's just a confused kid. He doesn't seem to understand much.'

'Yes, I'm serious. He might be a feral. Wouldn't be the first . . .'

Shortly afterwards, Sergeant Adams came back into the office. He sat down across from Ben again.

'That was Doctor Macreedie on the phone. He's my cousin – a good man. We were talking about you, Ben. You see, I don't really know what to do with you. There are procedures, of course. I could play it by the rule book.'

Ben met his look. 'What does that mean?'

'You're an unknown, Ben. You're either lying or suffering some kind of mental block. I believe it's the latter. I believe you're trying to tell the truth, but you're clearly confused and disorientated. You've had a shock and you need help. Correct procedure would have me on the phone to Social Services, arranging for a temporary care order. But I've had dealings with them before, Ben. You need help – you don't want to get caught up in a lot of red tape. I can't just hand you over to the Social. I want to do what's best for you. So I called my cousin, Tom Macreedie. He's a good man and a very fine doctor. He'll be able to help. He's said you can stay with him tonight. He'll make sure you're OK. You'll be much safer in the care of my family.'

'Feast nights can be wild, wild nights,' said

Doctor Macreedie. 'You're lucky my cousin found you when he did.'

Doctor Macreedie was a portly man, the shiny flesh of his neck bulging over a white collar, where a dark tie was pulled tight. He was sweating, as if nervous, and his dark eyes were never still behind tiny half-moon spectacles. Ben was in the passenger seat of the doctor's small hatchback. They had just passed a rowdy group of people emerging from one of the pubs on the high street.

'If you'd been out on your own much longer, you could have ended up anywhere. You'd be waking up in a ditch tomorrow morning, wondering what had hit you.'

'It's a feast night,' said Ben. 'I should have known.' But he didn't know anything.

Doctor Macreedie nodded. 'These nights were always the busiest when I used to work in Accident and Emergency,' he said. 'People with no self-restraint ... They get carried away nowadays. Children should be protected from over-indulgence. Sharing is a family thing. That's why you should have been safely at home tonight, Ben. Unfortunately, that view is not as widely held in the modern world as it once was. Listen to me – I'm preaching at you. I should have been a priest!' He chuckled. He was trying to put Ben at ease – and struggling.

Ben thought of Rachel, Stacker and Lenny this afternoon. What would Doctor Macreedie have made of what they did to each other? he wondered. Would he count that as 'over-indulgence' or would he dismiss it as youthful exuberance? Ben shuddered. How could he be thinking so calmly about his situation? Only a few hours ago he had been watching the football on satellite TV with his best friend. Now he was sitting in a stranger's car, being driven through a town that was not-quite-Kirby, where all the rules of life seemed to have been distorted . . .

The car swung into a driveway, its wheels crunching on gravel. It stopped before a red-brick building, with a modern, flat-roofed extension to one side. Ben undid his seatbelt and climbed out of the car.

The doctor's family were waiting in the doorway. His wife was a tall, thin woman, with dark hair tied tightly back from her face. She was carrying a toddler. All Ben could see of the child was its pale blue sleepsuit and mass of golden curls.

Its face was buried at its mother's neck. Its head was making steady suckling movements.

Ben saw that Doctor Macreedie was studying his reactions. He suddenly felt that this might be some kind of test and did his best to look blank.

'Ben,' said the doctor. 'This is Jillian, my wife, and our son, Adam – who should really be asleep by this time, but never is. He has more energy than the two of us! Adam will be two next month, won't you, Addie?'

The doctor reached out and his wife shifted their son. Where Adam had been suckling there was now a gaping red wound, slick and wet with fresh blood. The child's face was smeared with red, just as Lenny's had been this afternoon.

'Adam,' said Doctor Macreedie, taking his son and wiping his face with a moistened finger. 'Will you say hello to Ben? Ben will be staying with us for a while. We're going to be helping him. Jillian, would you boil the kettle?'

Little Adam peered over his father's shoulder. His tiny mouth twitched, revealing a crooked, gappy row of crimson-stained teeth. ''Ello,' he said. Then he chuckled and turned his face to his proud father. ''Ello.'

Ben barricaded himself in the room they had given him.

For half an hour he had eaten biscuits, drunk sweet weak tea and listened as Doctor Macreedie and his wife had made an effort at normal conversation. And all the time, Ben's thoughts had raced. The V-word. Vampires. That's what these people were. Lenny, Stacker and Rachel . . . the doctor and his family . . . the skinhead thugs in town. All of them.

Somehow Ben had walked into a waking nightmare. An entire world where this was normal. 'Feast nights' – he knew why they were called that now. Nights when it seemed that anyone out alone was seen as fair game. Those skinheads might have bled him dry if he hadn't escaped.

And now . . . now he was in an ordinary

family home, apparently safe, with a doctor, his wife and a child who sucked blood.

Jillian was a quiet woman. She rarely spoke more than three or four words together. At first Ben had thought that this might be a consequence of her husband's need to fill every silence with words. Then he began to wonder if it was something to do with the wound at her neck – had giving her blood to her child left her mentally as well as physically drained?

Adam on the other hand was full of energy. 'You have to get used to the boy,' Doctor Macreedie had said at one point. 'He's a handful at the best of times and he just doesn't sleep . . . Most two-year-olds should be in bed by this time, shouldn't they, Addie?'

The child had just chuckled, and resumed crawling at high speed around the big kitchen-diner where they were sitting.

Every so often, Adam would try to climb into Ben's lap, like a cat. But it wasn't the warmth of his lap that the child was after. One time Ben picked him up as he tried to climb and instantly the child's mouth had opened wide. Jillian had swept Adam away and put him to her own neck instead . . .

'You sleep,' Doctor Macreedie had said. 'We can talk in the morning.' And so Ben had gone up to his room and shut the door against the Macreedies and their sleepless toddler. He closed the window, which had been left half-open, and then he managed to wedge a chair against the door handle so it couldn't be opened from the outside.

He sat on the edge of the bed. He had to calm the thoughts that were rushing through his head. He had to try to think straight. He had to try to work out what on earth was going on.

What had happened? Everything had changed. No, that wasn't quite true – many things were the same. Some things had changed just a little, like the street names and the market square. And some things had changed dramatically – the industrial estate where the allotments should be . . . oh, and the vampires, of course.

It was crazy. It couldn't be true. But somehow, either the world had changed around him or he had side-stepped into a different world, which was a twisted, distorted mirror-image of the one he knew. He'd read stories of parallel universes, and worlds where history had taken a different course. Was this a world where something long ago had been different? A world where human beings had become . . .

Vampires. That word was wrong, he realized, but it was the only one he knew for what he had seen. These people weren't vampires like the ones in films and horror stories. They didn't need to avoid sunlight, unlike Count Dracula, and somehow Ben doubted that garlic or crucifixes would have much effect either. No, these were just normal people who happened to drink each other's blood, for some strange reason.

Would Ben become a vampire too if – when? – they drank his blood?

He knew it couldn't be long before someone spotted that he was different.

He lay back on the bed and stared at the ceiling. These people had never known anything different to this world. It was like alcohol, in a way. People here drank blood on feast nights and maybe at other times too. The doctor had spoken of over-indulgence so, clearly, some people drank it to excess, like Rachel and the skinheads he'd fled tonight. To these people such things were normal, they were everyday. To them, Ben must be the freak.

He wondered what they did with freaks in this world . . .

Protection

When Ben went downstairs the following morning Jillian and the child had already gone out. Avoiding him, he was sure. Maybe she didn't trust him around the child.

Or maybe she didn't trust the child around *him*.

'You're looking a wee bit brighter this morning, I see,' said Doctor Macreedie when Ben entered the kitchen.

The doctor poured him a cup of tea without asking. 'Cereal? Toast? I'm afraid I can't offer you a full cooked breakfast as my wife and I are vegetarians.'

Ben stared at him, trying to work out if he was joking or not. There was no sign of humour in the man's expression; it was just a half-apologetic statement of fact. He clearly didn't see blood-sharing as a form of eating or drinking.

Ben ate some bread with the tea.

'Are things any clearer now?' asked Doctor Macreedie after a short time. 'Are the memories of your life coming back?'

But that wasn't possible; Ben didn't *have* a life in this world. He shook his head. 'I have the memories all right,' he said. 'They just don't fit in with anything else.'

The doctor waited until Ben had finished his breakfast, then he gestured to the kitchen door. 'Come along,' he said. 'Come and see my office.'

Doctor Macreedie's 'office' was his surgery.

He led Ben through the house to a heavy wooden door, which he unlocked and swung open on to a small corridor. He ushered Ben through.

To the left there was an archway through to a waiting area. Padded chairs lined the edge of the room, gathered around a low table displaying a selection of magazines. On the walls there were posters about asthma, the dangers of smoking, and a range of common blood disorders. Smaller cards on a display board advertised a mother and toddler group, stress-management workshops, weekly meetings of something called the Purity League and other community events and services. Like so much that Ben had seen in the last day or so, it was familiar and yet subtly *changed*.

He looked out through the opened blinds and realized that the surgery was in the newer part of the building, the flat-roofed annexe.

'Through here, if you will,' said the doctor.

Ben turned and saw that he was being led into one of the consulting rooms. He went in and sat and Doctor Macreedie eased the door shut before seating himself behind his desk.

Again – so familiar!

All the normal equipment for testing blood pressure and so on were just as you would expect. There was a small basin with a rubber glove dispenser, an examination bed protected by a pull-down paper towel, gaudy paintings tacked to the wall which could only have been produced by young Adam . . .

Doctor Macreedie's fingers pattered on a

keyboard and he stared intently at a flat-screen on his desk. He paused then and turned to look at Ben, transfixed.

'You're not one of us, are you, Ben? That's why there are no records of you or your family.'

Ben looked at the man. His face was sympathetic, compassionate. Slowly, Ben shook his head.

'Sergeant Adams said he saw it straight away, but I didn't believe him at first. I didn't think it was possible that there could be a boy walking the streets who is not as we are. But he insisted. He persuaded me to take you in and see for myself. He told me you needed help. He was right not to hand you over to Social Services. Who knows where you might be by now, if he had done that?'

'What will you do?'

'I'm a doctor, Ben. I want to help you. You're in the best place here. Sergeant Adams was right to entrust you to his family.' Doctor Macreedie put a gentle hand on Ben's arm. 'I will keep you here, of course, under the protection of my family. We'll need to take precautions for your own safety though. You must not go out as you did last night – you're a temptation to others and you're a danger to your own self, wandering the streets like that. Don't worry, my boy, I'll look after you.'

The doctor slid open a drawer and reached inside.

Ben looked at little Adam's paintings on the wall. One showed a stick figure with an over-sized head. Its mouth had been painted a bright red. He looked back and Doctor Macreedie was placing a syringe in its plastic wrapper on the top of his desk.

'It's OK,' the doctor said in a calming voice.

He took Ben's arm and turned it, then slid the sleeve up. Removing an antiseptic wipe from a sachet, he cleaned the inside of Ben's elbow, leaving the skin cold and tingling. Then he reached for the syringe and removed it from its wrapping.

'It's OK,' he said again. 'There's no need to be alarmed. I just need to do some tests.'

He slid the needle into the vein and Ben ground his teeth to stop himself from crying out. Slowly, the collecting tube filled a deep red.

When he was done, the doctor sealed the tube in another plastic bag and attached a label. He smiled at Ben. 'That's it,' he said. 'All done.'

Back in the main part of the house, Ben sat down at the kitchen table. On the inside of his elbow there was a small circular plaster, which he could feel through the sleeve of his shirt.

He didn't know what to think. His feelings kept swinging from fear and doubt to surges of hope that this doctor might be a man he could trust. He hardly dared hope that he had really found protection in this evil world.

Already, the long-term consequences of his situation were flooding in – even if he was safe now, this secure haven could not last forever. The secret would get out.

But at least he had some breathing space. A chance to learn about this place and to try to work out how he could ever get back to his own world.

'How could it have happened?' he asked. 'I don't belong in this world. I don't understand what has happened to me.'

'There are stories of people like you,' said Doctor Macreedie. 'A failure in development, a genetic flaw. Sharing blood has many medical and social benefits. For most of us, to not share blood leads to physical deterioration, deficiencies, a weakening of the immune system. But for some . . . damage at some crucial stage of development, or maybe disease of some form or another, might block the desire to share. There have always been stories of wild people who suffer like that – we call them "ferals".'

Ben remembered hearing Sergeant Adams use that word when he was talking to the doctor on the telephone last night.

In answer to Ben's curious look, Doctor Macreedie continued. 'They are . . .' He seemed to be struggling for an appropriate word. 'People,' he finally said. 'People who walk and talk and could almost pass as normal and yet who do not have the capacity to share blood. I have never seen one until now.'

'You think I'm one of these . . . *ferals*?'

The doctor shrugged. 'It seems a likely explanation. Something must have happened to afflict your memory, Ben, so that you don't remember your origins. You must have wandered into Kirby in your confusion.'

'Are there ferals nearby then?' asked Ben.

'Only stories,' said the doctor. 'Every so often the local papers report sightings from Halton, Witheringhoe, Weeley Woods, Cottersett, but it's all hearsay and foolery, if you ask me. Or rather, that was what I had always thought until you appeared in our midst. I'm not convinced, even now. Your blood tests may tell us more about your origins when we get the results back.'

Ben's thoughts raced. So there were other people in this world who were like him! Suddenly things seemed to be improving – he had found protection and now he had learned that he wasn't as alone as he had thought . . .

Ben sat alone at the kitchen table. He sipped from the too-sweet tea Doctor Macreedie had made him and reached for another homemade biscuit. Outside, he could hear the nasal whine of a lawnmower, the occasional hum of a passing car. It all seemed so normal, so *familiar*.

The doctor had gone to answer the telephone and now Ben started to listen in. He didn't like to eavesdrop, but it was hard to avoid doing so.

'. . . Yes, yes,' Doctor Macreedie was saying. 'You must. You really must. It should be a family event – we should all share in this good fortune. I insist, and it would be rude of you to refuse.' His voice was light. He was joking with someone, enjoying himself.

'Yes, you were right, I'm telling you. A feral, just as you said.' There was a pause, then the doctor said, 'No, my blood-cousin, it's only right. You found it so it's only right that you should come and share. I took a sample of its blood today . . . Yes, yes, just a syringe-full. You should have seen the look on its face! I had to try it. It's sweet and raw and full of strangeness – like none I've ever tried. You have to come, my cousin. We should open a vein together. It's only proper. I think we should celebrate our good fortune, don't you think?'

Ben didn't move. Couldn't think straight. All his illusions were shattered. Yes, he had found protection, but at what price? And how long would he survive in the doctor's care?

Just then, Doctor Macreedie came back into the room, smiling. Ben looked at him. There was something just a little too eager in the doctor's manner.

'That was Sergeant Adams,' said Doctor Macreedie. 'He was asking after you. He's going to drop in this evening.'

Ben looked away. 'I . . . I think I'll go upstairs.'

Ben rose and went out to the stairs. Doctor Macreedie followed him all the way. When Ben went into his room, the doctor shut the door behind him. An instant later, Ben heard the scrape of a key in the lock.

He went over to the window and stared out across the garden. The flat roof was below but he was too high up to jump. He sat on the bed and tried to think.

Weeley Woods. Doctor Macreedie had said that some of the sightings of ferals had been from the woods. Barlow's Patch ran alongside the woods – that was where Ben had been when the change must have happened.

46

He had to get out of here! He had to get to Weeley Woods.

Maybe if there were real humans hiding out in the woods, they would be able to help him. Where did these people come from, after all? Maybe they had come through from the real world just as Ben had.

And maybe they would know the way back.

The Woods

It was quite clear to Ben that Doctor Macreedie was not a man of action.

Until the previous day, the doctor had found it hard to believe in ferals – he was quite unprepared for keeping one captive.

The sheet from the bed made a handy rope. Ben tied it to the radiator, and then swung his legs out of the window. The sheet wasn't long enough for him to reach the flat roof, but he used it to get down part of the way, to a height where it was safe to jump. He landed with his knees bent and immediately dropped into a low squatting position, suddenly fearful that the roof would collapse under his weight.

It was OK. With his back to the house wall, he edged along the flat roof to the back of the building. At the far end of the garden there was a wooden fence and then another garden.

He moved towards the front, but then heard the crunch of tyres on the gravel. Jillian and baby Adam must have returned from wherever they had gone so early this morning.

Voices came from the front of the house; the doctor must have gone to let his wife and child into the house, maybe to tell them the good news that they had their own supply of feral blood locked in the spare bedroom.

Ben took his chance. He went to the back of the house again and lowered himself down from the flat roof. He landed in a flower bed and looked around. All clear.

Cautiously, he moved away from the house. He would head for the back fence, stay out of sight. If he climbed it, he would be in the far garden. From there he could cut through to the street and slip away.

The garden path cut diagonally between flower borders before reaching the lawn and then the kitchen garden. Ben paused, looked back.

Doctor Macreedie had emerged from the back

door. He stood there, eyes wide, mouth hanging open, hand half-raised, pointing. It was as if that instant was frozen in time.

Then the doctor took a big step out of the house. 'Hey!' he said. He stopped and looked up at the open window, the sheet flapping idly in the breeze.

Ben ducked his head and ran.

He didn't see the trike until it was too late. His shin rapped painfully against the metal crossbar and he plunged forward. Flat on his face on the lawn, he looked back, saw the doctor advancing between the borders, a mad, triumphant smile plastered across his face. The man's mouth was still open, teeth showing. Anticipation? Blood lust?

Ben reached for the trike, turned it, pushed. It didn't go in a straight line, but his aim was good enough. The trike trundled right into Doctor Macreedie's path. His legs went from under him, his arms flailed and he went down heavily.

Ben scrambled to his feet and sprinted across the lawn, through the kitchen garden to the wooden fence. He jumped at it and managed to swing a leg on top before the flimsy wooden structure collapsed beneath him.

There was an old man tying flowers to supporting wire frames in the neighbouring garden. He looked up at Ben and cried out, startled at the sudden intrusion.

Ben straightened and then sprinted across the garden to the side of the house and then out into the street. Once he was clear of the garden, he had to force himself to slow down. He didn't want to draw attention to himself.

He wondered how much time he might have before Doctor Macreedie sorted himself out. Would he chase him or would he accept that he had lost him? Ben remembered the look on the doctor's face – the desperation. He didn't doubt that Doctor Macreedie would be after him.

He hurried, without running, keeping his head down, staring at the ground, as if that would stop people noticing him.

He reached Regency Road.

A small green hatchback turned the corner. Doctor Macreedie's car!

Ben stopped in his tracks, looked all around.

There was nowhere to run, nowhere to hide.

He relaxed. It wasn't the doctor's car at all. Just another green hatchback. The driver was an elderly woman, sitting hunched forward so that her nose was almost touching the top of the steering wheel.

At the top of Regency Road, Ben crossed over.

He felt much safer once he was heading through the scrubby wasteland he had always known as Barlow's Patch. He wondered what they called it here. As he walked, the sounds of the road fell away behind him. Soon the town was out of sight. The path was pretty much like the one he normally took to get to Andy's house. A single track, worn through the grassland by walkers, bicycles and the occasional horse. In the winter, stretches of the path could be ankle-deep in mud, but now it was dry.

The path cut through a blackthorn thicket, just as normal. It would be easy to think that everything that had happened to him was some kind of illusion. A dream, perhaps. Maybe, if he kept on along this path all the way to the village of Weeley, he would get to Andy's house and everything would be back to normal. But no, he knew it was foolish to think like that.

He wondered what his parents and friends must be thinking, what sort of fears they must have for his safety. He felt helpless and very much alone in the world, whichever world this was. But he had to keep going. His best chance of finding company and maybe beginning to understand what had happened was to find the ferals in Weeley Woods.

After about ten minutes, he turned off on to another path, smaller than the first, not so well used.

Soon he could see the dark fringe of the woodland's edge. He quickened his pace.

Darkness. Cool, refreshing shade. He was in the woods. He'd made it. A sudden fit of shuddering overtook him, and he had to lean against a tree for support. It was only now that he realized just how scared he had been; he'd been blocking it out, concentrating only on walking, on not being noticed.

He straightened. He had to pull himself

together. It was not over yet. He'd reached the woods, but what now? Doctor Macreedie had only said there had been *sightings* of ferals in Weeley Woods, among other places. Rumours. Gossip. What if he found nothing?

He stopped himself. He would gain nothing by thinking too far into the future. He was here now, in the woods. His immediate priority was to avoid being found.

And, of course, that was exactly what any feral humans would be trying to do too . . .

He knew he should try to be methodical – start from one side of the woods and work steadily across to the other.

But that wasn't possible. The woods covered a vast area, spreading out in a squashed horseshoe shape that wrapped part way around the village of Weeley, with a railway line cutting across one corner.

There were countless paths threading their way through the woods, but they twisted and turned, making it impossible to explore the area in any logical and methodical way. Some parts of the woods were blocked off by thick patches of thorny undergrowth. Others were fenced off to keep people away from the old quarry workings.

It was an ideal place to hide.

Ben followed a path into the heart of the woods. Every few minutes he stopped and stood quietly, listening. He reasoned that he couldn't see very far in the woods, but human sounds like voices might carry for some distance.

Other than the occasional sound of a train, and a dog barking in the distance, he heard nothing. There were plenty of signs that people had followed this path recently, but all the footprints in the mud could easily just be locals passing through. Did vampires go for strolls in the woods? Some of them had dogs to walk, so he supposed they probably did.

He realized that he didn't even know what he was looking for. Would feral humans have shoes even? Maybe he should be looking for the imprints of bare feet. Shut off from civilization, these feral humans might be savages. Perhaps that was why the doctor had been so fascinated by Ben . . .

By late in the afternoon, Ben was hungry and dispirited. He remembered watching television programmes about how you could survive in the wilderness, living off nature. They showed people scraping about for roots, gathering leaves that could be boiled into tea or soup, finding berries and mushrooms. It looked easy on TV. But, in reality, Ben had seen no mushrooms. The only berries he had found were a few hard green blackberries that were nowhere near ripe. He didn't know which plants were safe to eat and which would poison him.

Hungry or not, he would have to find somewhere to sleep. Remembering the programmes, he found a fallen branch and dragged it over so that it leaned against a tree. He should be able to balance smaller branches against it, and smaller ones against those, and so on until he had a shelter.

It didn't work like that though. The thing kept collapsing. He decided that it wasn't worth it. It looked like being a dry night in any case. He would just have to take his chances with the weather.

*

He found an open area where he could see the stars through a gap in the trees. The undergrowth was thicker here, and he was able to pull loose grass together with fronds of bracken to make a kind of nest for himself.

The vegetation broke the hardness of the woodland floor for a while, but soon Ben was uncomfortable. The ground felt hard and cold. His jacket would have helped him stay warm, but he'd lost that in Kirby. Although he was exhausted, sleep remained a long way off. He couldn't shake the images of the last two days from his mind. The bright red smears across Lenny's face. Rachel smiling at him, laughing. The man with PURE OF BLOOD where his eyebrows should have been and the stink of beer and smoke on his breath. Most disturbing of all was the eagerness in Doctor Macreedie's expression, the anticipation.

If Ben hadn't taken his chance to escape he knew it would be all over by now – the doctor and the policeman would have bled him dry.

Or perhaps not. Perhaps they would have held back, keeping him alive so that they could come back for more of his blood another time, and another . . . another . . .

Woodland noises broke through his dark thoughts. Scuffling and creaking sounds came from all around. The movement of the trees? The sounds of animals? At one point, a sudden yelping sound startled him out of not-quite-sleep. A fox, he decided. A badger, maybe. He wondered if the animals here drank each other's blood too or if it was purely a human thing.

Later, he woke to cool drops of rain on his face. Ben opened his eyes and stared up at the night sky. Clouds were hiding the stars and everything was pitch dark. He raised an arm and there was a sudden stabbing pain across his shoulders and back.

Cautiously, he rolled on to his side, his body aching from sleeping awkwardly on the woodland floor. He wiped the moisture from his face with the back of a hand, and paused to gather his senses.

Rising, he moved across into the shelter of the trees, stumbling on the uneven ground and the tangle of bracken and long grass. He leaned against a tree, then sat, but the ground was muddy and the wetness instantly soaked through the seat of his trousers.

He went deeper into the trees. He found another place to settle against a tree, testing the ground with a hand before lowering himself. He had no idea what time it was, but he sensed that there were still many hours until morning and he had a long, uncomfortable night ahead.

He hurt.

He hurt in his muscles and in every movement of his stiff, aching body. He hurt in his dry throat, with every breath, with every attempt to swallow. He hurt in the depths of his empty stomach.

He hurt.

Dawn's light had only recently stolen through the woods, and Ben had watched the steady emergence of shapes from darkness, of details etched into those shapes, and finally, of colour. Birds sang and he cursed their joyfulness. What right had they to be so comfortable in this awful wood when he was sore and damp and still so very tired?

Ben thought again of those survival programmes he had seen on the television, and he wished he had paid more attention. He was hungry, but he knew that his most pressing need was something to drink. Without water he would not last long.

He stretched his arms and legs, trying to free some of the night's stiffness from his body.

Back in the clearing, there were puddles from the night's rain and he squatted by one and looked into its muddy depths. He scooped some of the water out in a cupped hand and eyed the brown liquid. He stood, shook his hand dry and looked around.

The trees' leaves were shiny with moisture. He took one, pulled it over his open mouth and shook it, but only a drop or two of water fell. He licked the leaf, finding more of the moisture that way. He licked others, and then felt suddenly self-conscious and stopped. A clearing had formed where a tree had fallen, and now Ben found a puddle in a cleft in the horizontal trunk. The water was clearer and he scooped handfuls up to his mouth and drank gratefully.

When he had finished, he leaned against the trunk and gathered his thoughts. Would he be ill from drinking this water? he wondered. He had no choice though.

He looked around to find his bearings, then headed deeper into the woods.

Soon he came to the railway. Its steep, rocky embankment was ahead of him, cutting a straight line through the woods. There was a fence at the foot of the embankment – two strands of wire to mark the boundary between woods and railway property. The path followed the fence for a distance, and suddenly Ben remembered something his older cousin, Sophie, had once pointed out to him on a train journey to London: all along the track there were rambling apple trees, grown from the seeds in apple cores passengers had thrown out of train windows. He swung his legs over the fence and scrambled up the embankment.

Sure enough, a short distance along and part way up the slope, he came to an apple tree. The fruits were hard and green and he had to pull hard to snap them from their stalks. It was too early in the summer for them to be ripe, but even so he bit into one. It was hard and he found it difficult to break a piece off. It was dry and bitter too, but he managed to chew it, and to swallow, and he found that he wanted more.

He ate what he could of the apple and part of another, and then he stuffed more under-ripe apples into his pockets. Near to the top of the embankment, he listened. Hearing no trains, he crossed the track and scrambled down the far side into the shade of the woods again.

The woods were different here to how he remembered them. He began to realize that they must extend much farther to the north and west in this strange world. No wonder the so-called 'ferals' could hide themselves out here.

He walked, stopping often to listen, but all he ever heard were the sounds of the woods and the distant roar of the occasional train. It was a long day, and despite the apples in his pocket and the occasional clean-looking puddle of water, his hunger and thirst grew. It was stupid to think that he could find the ferals like this. Even if they really existed they would be well hidden. He might as well just call out at the top of his voice, asking them to come and get him.

But what alternative did he have?

He walked on, listening and looking for any signs that might indicate the presence of the ferals.

He stopped, late in the afternoon, tired and dispirited. He was thirsty again and his stomach burned with the sharp pains of indigestion brought on by unripe apples or bad water or probably a combination of both. He did not know what to do or where to go. He realized that he had a stark choice: stay here in the woods and possibly starve to death or return to Kirby to whatever fate Doctor Macreedie and his kind might have in store for him.

He did not know which was the better option.

The Wild Ones

It proved to be another uncomfortable night.

He found a tree with roots that spread wide at the base of its trunk, forming a hollow. At first it was comfortable to sit on a layer of the previous year's fallen leaves with his back against the trunk. Soon the hardness of the ground and the tree made themselves felt, as they had the night before, and Ben had to keep shifting, trying to find a position that was just a little less uncomfortable than the others.

As darkness crept furtively through the woods, Ben started to drift off to sleep, waking occasionally with an abrupt judder of his body and a racing of his heart.

At first, when he heard the voices, he was

convinced it was still a dream. His exhaustion had finally triumphed and he'd been dozing – and dreaming. In his dream he had been laid out on a hard stone bench in an operating theatre. Harsh lights shone down on him and his arms and legs were strapped tightly to the bench. He could hear people talking, but could see no one. And then a face loomed, close to his own: Doctor Macreedie, his mouth and nose hidden behind a surgical mask, his operating gown stained red like a butcher's apron.

'It's OK,' he said, in the dream. 'I'm a doctor. We just need to take a sample for a few tests.'

At that point in the dream, Ben was able to shift his head and look down at his own naked body. Coils of plastic tubing, red with his own blood, were attached all over his body with strips of surgical tape, and even then Doctor Macreedie drove another needle into Ben's belly, attaching another tube – transparent at first and then coloured a sharp crimson from within.

'It's OK,' Doctor Macreedie kept saying. 'It's OK.'

And all around, others mumbled and chanted,

their words impossible to make out. Words bouncing around inside Ben's head.

He opened his eyes. He could see the dark branches above him, silhouetted against the star-lit sky. He could still hear the voices, the words.

No! It wasn't the dream – it was people talking, somewhere nearby in the woods.

Suddenly, Ben was scared. What if the voices belonged to vampires looking for victims? Maybe they were searching for *him* – alerted by Doctor Macreedie and Sergeant Adams that there was a feral on the loose.

But the voices *could* belong to ferals. This was a chance he couldn't allow himself to miss. He climbed quietly to his feet.

Silence, then a gentle laugh, more low voices.

There were two of them, Ben guessed. They might be following one of the many tracks that criss-crossed the woods, but they could easily be following another, secret, route.

Ben stared in the direction of the voices. Should he confront them or should he try to follow them?

He would have to get closer, whatever he

decided to do. Perhaps if he was closer he would be able to make out what they were saying. Then it might be easier to decide.

He crept through the woods, treading as carefully as he could in the darkness. It was hard to move fast and stay quiet at the same time, and they were moving more quickly than Ben, getting ahead of him.

He kept going, not daring to move any faster in case they heard him. And then he realized that they hadn't spoken for some time.

He stopped.

He couldn't hear any sounds of them walking through the woods. No voices. Not even in the distance. Had they moved so quickly that they had left him far behind?

A sudden sound of footsteps nearby.

A voice. 'Following us, eh?' Someone grabbed a handful of Ben's hair and pulled his head back so that his face was tipped up, his throat exposed. He started to cry out, but a gloved hand smothered his mouth, trapping the sound. He felt a hard line against his throat. The blade of a knife.

The voice again, closer now. 'One false move and I slice you. OK? Maybe I'll slice you in any case. Give your kind something to feed on.' He chuckled.

For a few seconds rough hands searched him, patting down his body, going through his pockets. All Ben could see were the trees and the stars and part of the gloved hand clamped over his face.

'Come on, Robby,' said the man who was holding Ben. 'You kill it and the place'll be swarming with them.'

'Not if we dump it some place else. You mind it doesn't bite your hand.'

Instantly, the grip on Ben's face eased a little. 'I –' he gasped, but he couldn't say anything more.

There was a pause, then the man called Robby, who appeared to be the leader, spoke again. 'You should know not to come stalking us out here.'

'I –' Ben tried to speak again. The grip on his face eased and suddenly he could speak. 'I'm not one of them,' he gasped. 'I'm not a vampire.'

'A *what*? What are you talking about?'

Ben tried to think. In a world where blood-sucking was normal maybe they didn't need a special label – the townfolk weren't 'vampires', they were just *people*.

'I don't suck blood,' Ben croaked, struggling to speak with his head pulled back. 'I'm a feral. You've got to believe me!'

The gloved hand changed its grip and pulled Ben's mouth open wide.

'Maybe he's telling the truth,' said the man who was holding Ben.

'I don't know,' said Robby. 'It could be a trick. Just because he doesn't have the teeth for it, it doesn't mean he's not a beast. He talks like them and he uses their word for us – he calls us *ferals*.'

'I called you that because I've just escaped from them and that's the word they used.'

'So what are you doing out here in the middle of the night then?'

'I don't belong here. This isn't my world. I don't know why I'm here, but where I come from there's no such thing as . . .' He stopped and then started again, trying to explain. 'I came to the woods because they said that what they called ferals had been sighted here and I thought it was my only chance.'

The grip on Ben's hair eased and he was allowed to straighten.

There was a short man standing in front of him: Robby. He had long blond hair and was wearing a dark coat and what looked like jeans. There were bulging bags nearby.

The man saw Ben looking at them. 'Been foraging in town,' he explained. Then he added, 'That's a fancy story you tell. But what makes you think you can just walk in here like this? Do you think we're stupid? Listen, kid. My big friend here is going to let you go and we're going to point you in the right direction. You keep walking until you get to Kirby and you forget you ever came here, right?'

'But –'

'I should have sliced you right away,' said Robby. 'A lot easier all round.'

The second man released Ben and moved round to gather up the bags. He was tall and heavily built and he didn't want to meet Ben's look.

'They had me trapped in a room,' said Ben. 'A doctor and a policeman. They wanted to keep me so they could drink my blood. If I go back . . .'

The short man pointed back through the woods. 'That way,' he said. 'Seven miles to town.'

'They'll kill him,' said the tall man. 'And they won't do it quickly,' he added.

'I should have knifed him straight away,' said Robby softly. 'Come on then. But you walk in front of me, kid. I want to watch your every move.'

The People of the Woods

They walked until the sky was greying over with the first light of dawn.

The taller of the two scavengers, Zeb, led the way, setting a fast pace – deliberately, Ben suspected.

Ben fell several times, stumbling over roots and unexpected bumps in the ground. Each time he fell, Robby poked him with a booted foot, and told him to get up and walk.

After a time, the frequent twists and turns had made Ben lose all sense of direction and it was as much as he could do simply to keep up with the ferals. He guessed that they must be taking him on a roundabout and difficult route to their camp – a route so devious that he would lose his bearings and would never be able to remember it.

And then they were suddenly there; the encampment was all around them.

The narrow track they had been following had reached a dense barrier of holly. Ben thought the path just stopped, but ahead of him Zeb slipped through a parting in the dark green wall. Ben followed him through the gap.

They emerged in a clearing. The open sky and the early morning light made it a little less gloomy than it had been in the woods, but still it took several seconds for Ben's eyes to adjust. At first it looked pretty much like any other of the many clearings in Weeley Woods. Young trees forced their way up through tangled heaps of brambles and honeysuckle. There was running water – a stream, out of sight in the undergrowth. Then he began to make out the regular shapes of buildings. There were shelters scattered throughout the clearing. The brambles and honeysuckle had been trained to grow over them, disguising them from onlookers. Ben could hear hens somewhere, but he couldn't see where.

Robby pushed him in the back. 'Get moving, kid.'

At the centre of the clearing there was a grassy area that was free of brambles and shelters. Zeb and Ben waited there while Robby went to one of the nearby shelters.

Ben watched as the short blond man leaned into the doorway and spoke to whoever was inside. Seconds later, he backed away and a taller man emerged. He had shoulder-length black hair and a full beard that was flecked with grey. He was wearing loose brown trousers and a kind of cape wrapped around his shoulders. He walked across the clearing, staring at Ben and, without comment, reached round to the back of Ben's head and grabbed a handful of hair. Tipping Ben's head back, the man stared into his open mouth.

'Where are you from?' he asked in a deep voice. 'What are you doing here?'

The man released Ben's head. Ben straightened. He swallowed, his throat dry.

'I . . . I don't know,' he said. 'I don't know what happened, but I don't belong here. I escaped from Kirby. They had me locked up.'

The man grunted. His dark brown eyes never

left Ben's face. 'What are you doing here?' he repeated.

Other people were emerging from the shelters now. They must have heard the voices and realized that something unusual was happening.

'The doctor in Kirby said there had been some sightings of . . . of normal people . . . here in the woods. I didn't know where else to go.'

The man turned on Robby and Zeb suddenly. 'Why did you bring him here?' he barked.

Robby raised his hands defensively. 'We caught him following us,' he said. 'Didn't know what trouble he might cause us, roaming about in the woods like that.'

'What else could we do, Alik?' asked Zeb softly. 'Send him back to the beasts?'

Ben looked across at Zeb, grateful that at least one of these people was prepared to give him a chance.

'Quite right, Zeb,' said another voice. Everyone turned to see who had spoken. A stocky, grey-haired man stood in a gap in the undergrowth. He looked very ordinary, but there was a confidence in his words that made everybody pay attention.

'What would you have done, Alik? Send the boy back to provide wild blood for the beasts?'

Alik shook his head slowly. 'I wouldn't have put myself in that position,' he said. He turned to Robby and Zeb again. 'You're getting sloppy,' he told them. 'Bringing trouble into the community like this. Any mistake you make out there could be all it takes to lead the beasts right here. You'd better tighten up, you hear?'

The community hall was an impressive construction. It was built from corrugated steel, bent over to form a semi-circular tunnel that must have been five metres high and twenty or thirty metres long. The whole thing was so well disguised with ivy and brambles that even close up Ben hadn't realized how large the building was.

'This place used to be a farm,' said the older man. His name was Walter and he turned out to be Zeb's father. It was clear that he was some kind of leader in the community. 'The place was abandoned years ago. It seems appropriate to have taken it over and turned it to good use.'

Inside, the hall was gloomy and the air smelt of human bodies. There were maybe thirty people in there, and everyone stopped what they were doing to stare at Ben.

Walter waved a hand towards the far end of the hall. 'It goes right back under the trees,' he explained. 'We pipe water in from the brook and in the winter the families tend to move in here to share the warmth. The building has smoke traps in the chimneys, you see, so the beasts can't see the smoke from our fires.' Ben could smell cooking from the far end of the building and suddenly he felt sick with hunger.

In a louder voice Walter said to all the on-lookers, 'This is Ben. He's my guest.' He turned to Ben again. 'I expect you'll be hungry?'

Soon they were out in a small clearing in the early morning sun. Ben was tucking into a bowl of some kind of corn porridge, made from grain harvested at night from local fields. He'd already eaten two boiled eggs.

Walter watched Ben eat for a short time, then he said, 'OK, Ben. We've given you food and protection. Now it's your turn to pay us.'

Ben stopped eating, chilled by the man's words. He remembered breakfast with Doctor Macreedie, and the eager, hungry look on the man's face.

But Walter was smiling. 'You must repay us with your story,' he said. 'A stranger, lost in the woods – you must have quite a tale to tell.'

They listened as he recounted what had happened. Even Alik and Robby came to sit down and listen. When he told them about the doctor, he saw the looks of shock on the listeners' faces.

'He wanted to keep me locked up in his house,' Ben said. 'He wanted to keep me for his family. He didn't really seem to see me as a person at all; I was some kind of animal.'

'You were different,' said Alik, smirking. 'Exotic. I bet he couldn't believe his luck! He'll be cursing you now.'

'Family is important to the beasts,' said Walter. 'The doctor would have shared you with his "blood kin", as they call them. You were lucky to escape when you did. Once they've started . . .'

'The place where you come from,' said a young woman with red hair and a scarred face. 'What's it like, again?'

'It's . . . *safe*,' said Ben. 'You don't have to hide out in woods. People live in towns and cities and there's no such thing as . . . as what you call the beasts – except in stories where we call them "vampires". Only, the vampires in stories are different. They only come out at night, and they're frightened of crosses and garlic . . .'

'All just stories,' said Alik dismissively. 'If only the beasts were so easy to frighten!'

'It's like stepping into a mirror and out the other side,' said Ben. 'Things are so familiar here, but some things have been turned inside out. I've lived in a town called Kirby for the last six years, but not *this* Kirby.'

Ben looked up and saw a vaguely disappointed look on Walter's face, as if he didn't believe Ben's story. 'It's true,' said Ben. He had hoped these woodland people would be able to help him understand. He had hoped they might even know how to get him back to his own world.

But they didn't believe him.

For the first time he started to accept that there might be no way back.

Walter was nodding. 'You clearly believe that it's true,' he said. 'Let's leave it at that.'

'It's like the children's stories,' said the red-haired woman. 'Stories of worlds where things are different.'

'Only stories,' said Alik harshly, his tone ending all discussion.

How Things Are

For the rest of the morning Ben tried to sleep in the community hall, but despite his tiredness he couldn't settle.

When Ben emerged, Walter put him in the care of his son, Zeb. 'Show him around,' he told him. 'Teach him the ways of the community so he doesn't get caught again.' He didn't need to add: and so that he doesn't lead the beasts back here.

Around the middle of the day, the two of them were sitting on the railway embankment, leaning back on some rocks to soak up the sun. As far as Ben could tell, they were a few miles further north from the point at which he had first crossed the railway, but he couldn't be sure.

'You'd better watch yourself,' said Zeb in his soft voice. 'Everyone listens to Walter, but it's Alik that really makes things happen around here. If he doesn't want you here then you'd better be real careful.'

Ben remembered the feel of Robby's knife on his throat. 'Life must be hard out here,' he said, changing the subject.

'We manage,' said Zeb. 'There's a lot of natural food in the woods. Deer, rabbits, birds' eggs, fruit, mushrooms. We keep hens. We do some harvesting of local fields, too. As long as we don't harvest too heavily from any one field we're OK – a farmer sitting up on a combine harvester doesn't notice a few bare patches in his field. They don't notice a few cows milked at night either. Some of us go foraging in town when we can.' He patted his jeans and grinned. 'You'd think they'd learn not to leave clothes out on washing lines overnight.'

'How do you survive out here though? All it would take is a single mistake to lead them back to the community and it would all be over.'

Zeb shrugged. 'We're careful,' he said. 'The

woods are a big place and we make sure we don't give ourselves away. Anyway, I reckon some of the beasts like it that way – their own colony of ferals somewhere in the woods. Every so often one of us does make a mistake and gets caught. A bit of wild blood for the beasts, a bit of sport. Maybe they don't try too hard to find us – don't want to spoil their fun.'

Ben thought of how farmers in his own world left little corners of woodland and hedgerow alone for game birds and foxes to breed in. Was that why Weeley Woods appeared to be bigger here? Were the ferals conserved for sport?

Zeb glanced pointedly at Ben's jeans and sweatshirt, and at his smart new trainers. 'So how did you get here then if you're really from some other world . . . ?'

Ben looked away. 'I don't know,' he said. 'I was telling the truth, though. One minute I was *there* – walking home across Barlow's Patch. And then . . .' He remembered the storm, the sudden sense of rushing air, of being pulled apart. 'And then I was *here*.'

Zeb seemed to accept this and Ben felt a surge

of relief that this wild man of the woods didn't argue with his account.

'That's how it happened, is it? Just some freak accident?'

'I suppose so,' said Ben. 'All I know is that my world isn't like this. I don't know what happened, but somehow I ended up here.'

Zeb nodded, but said nothing.

Into the silence, Ben said, 'Thanks, Zeb.'

'Hmmm? What for?' Zeb looked awkward, uncertain.

'For speaking up for me – last night, and again this morning.'

'Oh . . .' Zeb shrugged. 'People are suspicious. Some of them reckon you're some kind of spy,' he said. 'But I told them if you were a spy you wouldn't come here in new, clean town clothes, would you? You stand out too much.'

Ben was about to ask why nobody but Zeb believed him, but he stopped himself. Why should they believe him? If someone had told him the same story a few days ago he would never have accepted it.

'I'm not mad,' he said. 'And I'm not lying.'

'Maybe,' said Zeb. 'But if you're not mad and you're not lying, what *are* you?'

Zeb was a good teacher, but Ben had a great deal to learn.

That first day, he led Ben away from the encampment. Once they were through the thick screen of holly, it was suddenly as if the camp had been imaginary. No sounds of people reached Ben's ears, and there was nothing to see that might indicate occupation. They might simply be strolling through the woods – out for a summer walk. For a short time, Ben allowed himself to accept that fantasy, but he knew it was not true. The tall man he followed wore a coarse cape across his broad shoulders unlike any clothing familiar to Ben from his own world.

They walked for some time along a narrow trail that could easily be taken for an animal track. Along the way, Zeb pointed out the different kinds of trees and plants, pausing occasionally to indicate animal – and human – tracks in the mud. All the names of the plants and animals, one after another . . . Ben knew he would never remember.

Eventually they came to a rest.

Zeb looked at him closely. 'OK,' he said. 'Where are we?'

Ben shrugged, unsure of the correct response.

'An easier one – which direction back to the camp?'

Ben turned, but he realized that the twists and turns of the trail had fooled his sense of direction and he had not been paying enough attention to their route to have a satisfactory answer. He shrugged again. 'I . . . I followed you,' he said feebly.

Zeb's eyes narrowed. 'Perhaps I should just leave you here then,' he said. 'If I was Robby that's what I'd do.'

Ben looked at him and he knew that he might easily do just that. Despite his kindness there was something edgy about Zeb, a wildness that was more animal than human. Survival was instinctive for these people, and the safety of the community would always come a long way ahead of Ben's welfare. They wouldn't hesitate to sacrifice him if they had to, even Zeb.

'Walter asked you to teach me the ways of the

community,' Ben said. 'If I learn how to survive out here then I'm less risk for all of you.'

Zeb nodded. He took Ben by the shoulder and turned him to one side. 'North,' he said. 'See the algae on the tree trunks? It grows best in the shadow on the north side of the tree.'

Sure enough, the green smudges on the bark of the nearest trunk were more dense on one side.

'If you're in doubt, listen for the trains. You can always get your bearings from the direction of the trains.'

Zeb didn't let up until the evening started to close in.

They ate with Walter and some of the others, and gradually Ben began to learn the names and relationships of the people he had joined.

And that night he slept. He was warm and dry and he felt safe. Even the floor of the big community hall didn't seem so hard as he settled down next to one wall and closed his eyes.

When he woke his body hurt with all the muscle-pain and stiffness he had come to expect from sleeping on a hard floor, and yet somehow it did not seem to matter. He felt as safe as he had ever felt in this strange world and there was a chance – however slim – that these people might accept him. Walter had offered him the woodlanders' protection. Zeb had started to show him the ways of feral life. He recognized the strange feeling that he had woken with this morning – it was hope.

Out in the clearing, one of the women waved him over to join a small group and a young girl handed him a carved wooden bowl filled with steaming corn porridge.

A short time later, a small boy with shaggy, shoulder-length hair said, 'Will you tell us again? Will you tell us what you told us again?'

Ben hesitated, but all seven of the children had turned to him now. 'OK, OK,' he said, laughing, as an excited chatter broke out around him. 'I'd been to see a friend and I was walking back across Barlow's Patch. There was a big storm building up and it started to –'

'No! Before that!' cried the girl who had given him the porridge. 'Tell us about the world where there aren't any beasts.'

He stopped, and thought.

He thought of his parents, of Stacker and Arthur and Gav, of the skateboard park and the after-school football knockabouts.

'I . . .' He didn't have the words. It hurt even to think about all he'd lost. 'It's just a normal world,' he said. 'People like us – we live in houses, in towns and cities. We go to school. There are good people and there are bad people, but there are no beasts. It's –'

A sudden commotion cut him off in mid-sentence as Robby pushed his way into their midst. Suddenly Ben was sprawling in the dirt. His ribs throbbed where Robby had kicked him.

Tears and grit stung his eyes as he peered up at his attacker. Ben held his arms out in a feeble attempt to defend himself.

Robby had a knife – probably the one he had held to Ben's throat not so long ago. He stood over Ben now, looking at him along the length of the blade. 'You've been told,' he said in a low voice. 'We've heard enough of your lies and stories. Are you listening? You start stirring up trouble and you'll regret it.'

Zeb came then. He put a hand on Robby's back and said something in his ear. Robby glowered at him, then turned and walked away.

Zeb leaned over, offering Ben a hand.

Ben stood and brushed himself down. His ribs still throbbed where Robby had kicked him. He noticed that the children who had been listening to him had all been shepherded away by one of the adults.

'You need to watch out,' said Zeb, smiling awkwardly, trying to reassure Ben. 'Stories can be dangerous things if people start believing in them. You should keep a low profile. Some people don't think we should have taken you in, and they don't want you telling stories you don't understand.'

Stories. That's all his words were to most of the woodlanders. 'Do you believe me, Zeb?'

'You're not one of us,' said the tall woodlander. 'So you must have come from somewhere else. I don't believe and I don't disbelieve, but what I do know is that you're here and you have a lot to learn. If you want to survive out here then you need to stop stirring up trouble – forget about whatever went before and concentrate on *now*, OK?'

Ben nodded.

'Come on.' Zeb turned and walked away. Ben followed, and soon they had left the settlement behind.

They walked some distance in silence and then paused in a patch of sunlight. Zeb touched Ben's arm and pointed. Ben tried to see what it was that he was indicating and then he realized that he was alone – Zeb had used that moment of distraction to vanish.

Panicking, Ben recalled their first trip out into the woods when Zeb had appeared to consider abandoning him. He calmed himself and looked around, hoping for some sign of where his companion had gone. He listened, but heard nothing that helped him.

And then a hand fell on his shoulder.

Ben twisted, gasping, ready to flee, until he saw that it was only Zeb.

'You have to be able to conceal yourself at an instant's notice,' Zeb said patiently. 'And you have to be able to move silently.'

Ben shook his head, amazed at how Zeb had so easily deceived him.

'Which way to the camp?' Zeb asked.

Immediately, Ben pointed through the trees.

Zeb clapped him on the arm. 'You're learning, you see?'

Ben grinned. 'But I still have a long way to go, right?'

On the way back, they came to a point where their narrow trail crossed a broader path and suddenly Zeb plucked Ben's arm and pulled him into cover.

Ben peered at him in silence. He listened, but heard nothing out of the ordinary.

Then, after a short time, he heard voices. A man, a woman. Walking along the path. Ben looked at Zeb and saw him nod.

Beasts.

They hid and waited. It was easy to forget what a dangerous world he now inhabited.

The Old Man in the Woods

'I'd like you to meet someone, Ben,' said Walter. 'I think he might help you.'

Ben had been with the woodland community for three days now, spending his days with Zeb and his nights sleeping on the hard floor of the community hall. Slowly, he was learning how to find his way around, how to hide himself and conceal his tracks, what was safe to eat and what was poisonous. At times he felt that he was making good progress, but at others he still felt out of his depth – lost in a strange world.

He lived in the present, each day an achievement, another day survived. He tried not to think about what he had left behind and he dared not think too far ahead about what might come. He just tried to learn and to fit in.

'Where are we going?' he asked Walter. The community leader took him under the dark canopy of the woods, away from the brook where Ben had been helping two young women, Anna and Rose-Marie, to prepare some long stringy roots that Rose-Marie's grandmother would boil down into a medicinal paste. While they worked, they'd been listening to the radio, the volume turned low – at first, strange music, and then a drama, which seemed to revolve around who it was polite to share blood with.

'I want you to meet Old Harold,' said Walter. 'He's one of the wisest people I know. Must be about seventy years old. Lived alone in the woods all his life. He doesn't talk to the rest of us very often, but I keep an eye on him – listen to his tales and make sure he's all right. I think you have a lot in common with him, Ben.'

Old Harold lived in one of the oldest trees in the woods.

Walter and Ben had left the path some time ago. Now they were threading their way through a tightly packed thicket of young trees, spread over the gentle slope of a hill.

'This area was felled some time ago,' Walter explained. 'They were going to do some quarrying, but for some reason it was abandoned and the trees grew back again like this. Harold says he likes it because it's full of nightingales in the summer.'

After a time, they reached the far end of the young growth and soon they came to Old Harold's tree. It was an oak, and its bark was near-black and ridged and knotted into endless patterns. The trunk was hollow and if there had been an opening big enough you could probably have parked a small car inside.

'Harold,' said Walter, poking his head into a crack in the trunk. His voice echoed inside the hollow tree. 'I've brought Ben. I've brought the boy we talked about yesterday.' He stepped up on to a raised root and then clambered through the cracked trunk and dropped inside.

Ben followed him. It took a few seconds for his eyes to adjust to the darkness. Inside, the tree had been carved out to resemble a small room; there were shelves lined with jars and books, seats cut out of the wood, a long, low shelf where Ben suspected the old man slept.

A spiral of narrow steps wound up around the inside of the hollowed trunk. Ben's eyes followed their course and then he noticed a face protruding into the circle of light above them. It was an old man, with white hair tied back with a leather band and a thick beard that had been twisted into a series of little pig-tails.

There was a pause, then the man said, 'Come on up, lad. Come into the light where I can see you.'

Walter turned. 'I'll leave the two of you,' he said. 'You can find your way back, can't you, Ben?'

Ben nodded. It was the first time he'd been left without a chaperone since he'd come to the woods. Perhaps they were learning to trust him now.

He climbed the tiny steps, holding on to any handholds he could find. Old Harold must be very agile to use steps like these.

The old man was sitting on a bench cut into dead wood where the tree branched out from its enormous trunk. He was wearing a cloak, as many woodlanders did, and his bare knees thrust out from underneath it to provide a resting place for his chin.

Ben settled down next to him. From this view-point he could see out across the tops of the younger trees to the main bulk of the woodland. The trees seemed to roll away for miles and miles until they were finally lost in the distance.

'The boy from another world,' said the old man, after a long silence.

Ben peered at him, not knowing what to say. The old man was studying him closely.

'You make them uncomfortable with your stories,' said the man. 'Your claims of a better world. They tell stories like that to the children, but they don't believe. If they believed such a thing, then they would despair because they are here and not there. Do you see what I mean? You frighten them, Ben. That's what Walter wants me to explain to you. He doesn't want you damaging the community with your stories.'

Ben had already worked that out – ever since Robby's attack he had stopped telling people about his world. He nodded. 'I know,' he said. 'But I had to tell them. I had to find out if they knew how to get back.'

'Back,' said Old Harold. 'Back to another world that only exists in the stories we tell our children.'

'I'm not mad,' said Ben stubbornly.

'Not mad, perhaps,' said Old Harold. 'But you believe things that cannot be true.'

'If my memories aren't true, then where have I come from? How did I suddenly appear here?'

'You've had a frightening experience,' said Old Harold. 'Walter tells me you were held prisoner by the vampires. Who knows where you have come from? You've blocked your memories out and filled them in with stories told to you as a child – a magical, safe world, where there are no vampires to hold you prisoner. It's a natural thing to do, Ben. You're not the first person to go through this.'

Ben shook his head. 'It's true,' he said. 'I don't belong here.'

'But you are here,' said Old Harold patiently.

'And you are not in the hands of the vampires. You should, at least, be thankful for that.'

The old man's voice was strangely soothing, convincing.

'The stories,' Ben said. 'I don't remember any stories. All I remember is living in a world that is not like this.'

'There are many stories,' said Old Harold. 'They get changed about and mixed up in the re-telling, as all stories do. We tell of worlds where everything is different. We tell our children of worlds where there are no vampires, Ben. Just the same as you tell. We tell of passages between this world and a safer one.'

He held his hands up, their backs turned to Ben, fingers spread. He moved them together so that the fingers interlocked. 'We tell of worlds so close together that they are almost the same place, of passages between worlds where the two fit together. All stories. Fantasy. Sometimes a vampire from this world enters the safe world and causes terror. We use that story to frighten children, to remind them that the world is dangerous after all.'

Passages between the worlds, universes over-lapping like the gnarled old fingers of Harold's hands. What if it was true? Could that explain how Ben found himself here? A place where two worlds overlapped. Maybe that was where the vampire legends in his own world came from?

'Sometimes we tell a story where one individual has special powers – a sensitivity. That person can find the special places where the two worlds brush close together and he or she can use this talent to open up a passageway between the worlds. That story gives hope. It suggests that there is always something better that we may achieve.

'We use the stories in many ways, Ben. We use them to entertain and we use them to teach our children important lessons about the world. But they are always just that – stories.'

'But it's true,' said Ben. 'It happened to me.'

'So you are the special one, are you? You are the individual who can find a way between the worlds?'

Perhaps. Or perhaps he had just stumbled

through by accident, when the passageway had been open – a freak natural event.

'You said I'm not the first to go through this,' said Ben. 'Are there others who have made the same claims? Are they all fooling themselves with stories from their childhood?'

Old Harold nodded. He leaned forward so that his head was inches from Ben's. 'There have been others, Ben. I was one of them. That's why Walter asked me to explain it to you – because I know what it is like to believe the unbelievable.'

Ben stared at him in surprise. 'You?' he gasped. 'You've been through this and you still tell me it's not true?'

Old Harold nodded again. 'I was young,' he said. 'About ten years old. I wasn't as lucky as you, Ben. I don't know what happened to me, but I was wandering around the countryside, lost, when I was picked up by a vampire. He kept me locked in his coal cellar for weeks. There's a very fine line between life and death and that monster kept me clinging to that line for all of that time. I had barely enough blood in my body to survive. I can still remember the terrible tiredness – I could barely move at times. And the pain, and the awful fear.

'For some reason the vampire left me alone for several days. I started to recover and I realized that this might be my only chance. I worked and worked at the hinges on the door until one came adrift. The door twisted on the bolt and the remaining hinge, and I was so thin I could force my way through the gap.

'I ran and I walked and eventually I crawled and by chance I ended up in the woods and was found by the woodlanders. I've never left this place since.'

'Where had you come from before the beast caught you?'

'I don't know,' said Old Harold. 'But for a long time I told people I had come from a world where there were no vampires, where there were no beasts like the one who had locked me in that cellar and drunk me almost dry. I was fooling myself, Ben. I didn't have anything else to believe, so I decorated my past with stories from my childhood.'

'How can you say that when you've just told me what you went through?'

'Because it's true,' said the old man.

Just then a thought struck Ben. 'You call them "vampires",' he said. 'That's what we call them in my world.'

Old Harold tipped his head on one side and thought. 'Vampires, beasts – what does it matter? What matters is what they do to you.' He paused, then explained. 'When Walter came he told me they'd found a boy who ranted about vampires. It's years since I'd heard that old word. I reckon it's what we called them when I was a boy. Took me back to when I was a kid, all the terrible things that happened. Can't remember when we started just calling them beasts. Long time ago, I reckon. They still suck your blood though!'

He put a comforting hand on Ben's back. 'Do you see what I'm saying to you, son? I never came from another world because there *is* no other world, only this one. I know you don't believe me, Ben. I know you probably hate me for trying to tell you that you are mistaken.

'But you will believe me, Ben. You really will.

You need to accept the truth if you are to survive in this harsh and unfair world of ours.' He waved a hand to indicate the broad expanse of woods. 'You need to accept that this is all we have.'

Foraging

Ben walked back alone from Old Harold's tree-house. There were so many competing thoughts in his head that he no longer knew what he really believed. He thought of how terrible it was that Old Harold had been through the same experience as Ben and that, so long ago, he had given up believing in the existence of his own world. But what if what the old man had said was true? That this was all there really was . . .

There was a sound from up ahead. Voices.

Instantly, Ben melted into the undergrowth, hiding until he was sure it was safe to go on.

This life seemed so natural to him. The thought came as something of a shock, but it was true. It was as if Zeb had spent the last three days *reminding* Ben of the ways of caution and fear, rather than *teaching* him.

The voices faded away and Ben stepped out from hiding. He decided to keep clear of the main paths on his way back, just to be sure.

Was it really so easy to fool himself? He couldn't believe it. He had to hang on to his past. He wouldn't give up like Old Harold.

And then an awful realization struck him – the details of his memories were fading. He had only been in this awful upside-down world for a few days, yet it felt as if he had been here for far longer. When he tried to picture his bedroom, all he could see was that room where Doctor Macreedie had imprisoned him. When he tried to picture Kirby town centre, all he could see was the market square with parking spaces and the beasts coming out of the shops to stare. And when he tried to picture his parents, he couldn't do it ... The memories were fading – if they really were memories at all, and not just figments of his own imagination.

He lay on the hard floor of the community hall

that night, still struggling to remember, still struggling to come to terms with things.

This was his world, he realized. Whatever had happened in his past, this was all that was on offer. It was a dangerous and frightening place, but he had found himself a community. Some of the people were good and some were not so good. Some of them hadn't accepted him yet. Robby was one – always looking for conflict, always looking for ways to remind people that Ben was the outsider. Perhaps more dangerous though was Alik: a powerful figure in the woodland community. He didn't trust Ben, he didn't think he should have been allowed to stay.

But others seemed more ready to welcome him: Walter, Zeb, Rose-Marie and her frail old grandmother. Walter had decided that the best thing was to make sure Ben learned the ways of the woods, which was why he had told Zeb to look out for him. They treated Ben as a young adult here, rather than as just another child. If there was one thing in this world that he liked, then that was it. He supposed people grew up more quickly, living in a world like this.

He tried to stop himself thinking in these terms – comparing this world with the safe world in his memories. He would gain nothing by thinking that way. This was his world, now. This was all he had.

A noise broke the darkness. The soft tread of feet.

Peering through the gloom, Ben made out a tall figure. Zeb.

The young man came across and squatted by Ben. 'Good,' he said. 'You're awake. Dad thought you might like to come foraging tonight. See a bit more of the world.'

Ben swallowed. 'Sure,' he said. 'Where are we going?'

'McDonnell's farm. About two miles east, on the edge of a small village called Tippham.'

Ben knew the name. He climbed to his feet.

Outside in the dark, four others were waiting: Anna and Rose-Marie and two teenage brothers Ben barely knew, Rick and Adam. Anna led the way and they walked in silence for some time.

Eventually, Adam spoke to Ben. 'All you have to do is stay quiet and stick close to the rest of us,' he said. 'We take whatever we can and we don't take any big risks. OK?'

'Of course,' said Ben. 'What are we looking for?'

'You never know,' said Zeb. 'The only rule is we never take too much of anything. Things we can carry, and things we can't come by easily in the woods, like clothes and tools, are best. Electrical things too – anything we can sell.'

'Sell? To the beasts?'

'There's always a black market,' said Rose-Marie. 'Alik and some of the others know where we can shift some of the things we forage. They exchange them for medicines and other supplies we can't get hold of for ourselves.'

It hadn't occurred to Ben that there could be anything like that going on. It made sense, he supposed. But it seemed very dangerous.

'How do they manage that?' he asked. 'How can you trade with the beasts?'

'Some of them are too stupid to even realize,' said Rose-Marie. 'You've been close to them, haven't you, Ben? They can't just sniff us out, you know. If you don't make any stupid mistakes you can go into town and not be noticed. I've done it myself when I've had to. We all have.'

Ben could tell from her voice that she was boasting, probably not telling the truth. But what she said was certainly possible. After all, Ben had walked around Kirby without being found out. He had stayed a night in the Macreedies' house before the doctor had been sure of his true nature.

'Quiet now,' said Zeb. 'We're nearly there.'

A short time later, the path opened out and there were fields to one side. A line of bungalows stretched along the far side of the field. Some had one or two lights on, but most were in darkness. This must be the village of Tippham.

Now Ben remembered what it was like to be scared, what it was like to know that you were only a single mistake away from a slow and painful death. Suddenly, all his other worries melted away. All that concerned him right now was remembering all the things Zeb had taught him – how to move silently, how to hide yourself from prying eyes, how to avoid being caught . . .

*

They came to McDonnell's farm a few minutes later. The farmhouse was an imposing red-brick building with stone columns at the front door and wooden shutters at the windows. There were lights on and several cars pulled up in the main yard.

'Looks like there's a party going on,' said Adam. 'Looks like we picked a bad night.'

'We're here now,' said Anna. 'The least we can do is look around.'

The farmhouse was surrounded by big, low outbuildings. Some were rectangular barns, others were arched buildings made from corrugated steel, like the community hall back in the woods.

As they drew closer to the farm, Ben heard animal noises coming from these buildings. 'What is it?' he asked. 'What's in there?'

'All kinds of things,' said Anna. 'Mainly pigs. Some cattle. Stables for horses – they have some kind of riding school.' She paused, then said, 'See the barn? The one with a tractor in the doorway? Alik asked us to look in there. See if there are any tools we can lift. Come on.'

They split up in the main yard. Rose-Marie, Adam and Rick headed towards the back of the building to see what they could find. Ben followed Zeb and Anna towards the barn.

Inside, there was another tractor and lots of attachments for ploughing and harvesting. Ben didn't know what it all was. He was a town boy, after all.

He stopped, shuddered. He *wasn't* a town boy. He lived in the woods. He was a wood-lander now, whatever the truth of his past.

The other two had found a store room. They waved Ben over.

'Here, wrap the blades in these.' Zeb handed Ben some rags and pointed to a selection of chisels and saws he'd taken from a tool cabinet.

Ben set to work, wrapping the cutting edges so that the tools could safely be put in a sack and carried back to the woods.

Somewhere nearby a horse whinnied.

The three finished wrapping the tools. Then Anna gathered up the sack and slung it over her shoulder. 'See you later,' she said.

Ben watched as she headed off across the

farmyard towards the woods. It made sense, he supposed: she would gain nothing by hanging around to wait for the others.

'Come on,' said Zeb.

Ben went with Zeb to a door at the back of the barn. It was open a crack and they could see through to the side of the farmhouse. The windows were open and voices spilled out into the mild summer night. Occasionally, a figure moved across a window. It all looked so normal.

'Keep watch,' said Zeb. 'I'm going to look around a bit more, see what else I can find.'

Ben was alone.

He wondered if this was some kind of plan – maybe Alik had told them to lead him away from the woods and abandon him. But every so often, he heard a small sound from the depths of the barn and he knew Zeb was not far away.

A horse whinnied again. From what Ben could see, the back of the barn butted on to some stables. Anna had said they had a riding school here.

He eased the door open a little wider. There

seemed to be a faint light coming from the stables. Was there someone in there?

Ben slipped outside. If he stayed close to the back of the barn, he would be in darkness.

He edged his way along towards the stables.

The doors were split, the top half open, the bottom closed.

He reached the stables and stepped towards the door.

A head and shoulders suddenly appeared in the opening. 'Wha–?'

Ben froze. He was in the shadows still. Zeb had taught him that movement attracts the eye; stand without moving and you can be near invisible.

A bright light shone in his face.

'*You*,' said a girl's voice. 'What are you doing here?'

He recognized the voice. The light flicked out and, for a moment, Ben was still blinded. Then his vision returned and he saw that she had emerged from the stables, clutching a saddle to her chest.

It was the girl from town. The one with the spiky blonde hair and the tight jeans.

Rachel. That was her name. She'd been with the two boys.

She'd let them drink her blood.

Ben started to back away.

She stood there, smirking at him.

And then there was another sound – a sudden swell of noise from the house as a door opened.

'Rachel?' called a man. 'Is that you out there, Rachel?'

There was a middle-aged man standing at the open door. He looked as if he was about to come right out.

Rachel looked from the man back to Ben again. 'It's OK,' she called. 'It's me, Dad. I'm just finishing.'

As the man went back into the house, Ben edged away, then turned and darted into the barn.

Zeb was by the far door, ready to run. When he saw Ben, he hurried over to him.

'We'd better go,' hissed Ben. 'There's someone outside at the stables.'

'Right. OK. Let's go.'

'Did you find anything else?'

Zeb collected a pickaxe he must have left by the big barn doors. He handed it to Ben and stooped again to pick up a petrol can. 'Just these,' he said. 'Come on, let's go.'

Rachel

He saw her again, briefly, about a week later. She was out riding a pony on one of the wide tracks that cut through the eastern side of the woods. He was with Zeb and the two of them hid in the woodland edge as the horse and rider swept by.

She looked peaceful and relaxed, just her and her pony and the trees. She looked normal. But she wasn't, Ben knew. That memory of her and the two boys would be imprinted on his mind for the rest of his life.

The next time he saw her was one of the rare occasions when he was on his own.

He'd been in the woodland community for two weeks now, and they still didn't fully trust him. Half the people thought he was mad – a boy with no past, or with no past that anyone would believe. The others thought he was lying, covering up something in his past that he didn't want them to know about. But they were unanimous in not trusting him. Walter had been more sympathetic than a lot of the woodlanders, but Ben realized that even he was suspicious. He didn't know if Walter thought him mad or a liar, but after a while he came to understand that Walter had asked Zeb to both look after him and keep an eye on him.

Zeb, himself, seemed to have accepted Ben now and he was far more relaxed than he had been at first. 'You've just got to forget about what may have been,' Zeb had told him on more than one occasion. 'What's past is gone. You just need to earn people's trust now.'

One of the reasons Zeb was more relaxed these days was that he clearly had other things on his mind. That morning Zeb had said to Ben hesitantly, 'Hey, Ben. You don't mind if Rose-Marie tags along with us this time, do you?'

Ben watched them together – the little looks, the way they walked so close together that they kept touching, the space between him and them.

'How's your grandmother?' he asked Rose-Marie, filling yet another silence.

'She's having a good day, thanks,' said Rose-Marie. 'Complaining about the food, which is a good sign.'

Silence again. Ben took the opportunity to study Rose-Marie as they walked. Her flame-red hair always caught the eye, but it was her easy smile that stayed in the memory. Ben had felt that she was intruding at first, when Zeb had invited her along. Now he realized that her presence was a good thing: Rose-Marie was well-liked in the woodland community and her acceptance of Ben could only have a positive effect. In Zeb and now Rose-Marie he had two good allies.

The three headed out towards Tippham Lakes, a series of three connected lakes on the east side of the woods. Rose-Marie's aging grandmother was teaching her how to use traditional herbal medicines, and the wet woodland around the lakes was good for some of the plants she wanted to gather.

After a time, Ben paused and said, 'Why don't

you two go on ahead? I'll be OK on my own. We can meet up here again at noon, if you like.' It was a chance to prove that their trust in him was good judgement.

Zeb and Rose-Marie grinned back at him. 'Sure,' said Zeb. 'If that's what you want.'

Ben watched as the two of them strode on through the alder wood. When they thought they were out of sight they held hands. Ben followed a narrow path that led up a slope, away from the lakes. He didn't know what to do with himself. It was just a relief not to have someone watching over him.

He wondered how much longer Walter would have him watched.

Rachel was sitting on a fallen tree in a small clearing. Her grey pony was tied up to a branch, its head down, munching at the rich green grass. Rachel was carving some letters into the exposed white wood of the tree trunk.

Ben hesitated. He should turn round and slip quietly back into the woods, he knew. It was foolish to even think of anything else.

She saw him watching her. 'Hello again,' she said. She didn't seem too bothered by his presence. 'New Boy.' That's what she'd called him, all that time ago in town.

'Hi,' he said. 'I was just –'

'Just passing,' she finished for him. 'Like the other night, just passing. When we met you in town I didn't think you approved of nicking things, the way you looked when we said that's what we'd been doing.'

He shrugged.

'But then you come with your mates, nicking stuff from the farm.'

'You could have said I was there,' he said. 'You had the chance.'

She nodded. 'I should have, I reckon. What did you want with all that stuff anyway? Old tools and things.'

And then her expression suddenly changed. 'Oh! Oh my . . . You *are*, aren't you? Lenny said you were. He said that's why you ran away. I just thought you were scared of us, mummy's boy – won't share blood with just anybody. But you are, aren't you? You're one of them – a feral!'

He started to back away.

She raised her hands in some kind of peace gesture. 'No,' she said. 'Don't run away again. It's OK. I'm not going to bite!'

She giggled, then stopped.

'Really, New Boy. It's OK. I won't tell anybody. I won't do anything. Don't run away.'

'My name's not New Boy,' said Ben. 'It's –'

'Piggy,' said Rachel. 'I'll call you Piggy, OK?'

'Have you lived in the woods all your life?'

'Where do you live?'

'Are there many of you?'

'What do your kind eat?'

'Do you still fancy me?'

And, in a weak voice, 'Oh my God, you really *are*, aren't you? A walking, talking feral! You really are, aren't you?'

Rachel was full of questions. He realized she must be lonely, living out in Tippham. From what she told him, she had no brothers or sisters and most of her friends lived in town.

He avoided most of her questions. He wasn't stupid enough to tell her where the community was or to tell her anything that might lead people there. He shouldn't be talking to her at all, he knew. But she was curious about him, and she was funny and suddenly it felt good to be with someone who didn't seem suspicious of everything he said and did.

'I haven't been here long,' he told her. 'A couple of weeks or so. I'm just hiding out here while I work out what to do.'

'Where are you from then, if you're not from here?'

He looked away. He didn't want to start all that again – the disbelief, the suspicion. She might just laugh at him if he told her, and that would be even worse.

'What's it like?' he asked her. 'Your kind. What you do to each other.' He didn't know how to put it into words. It would sound stupid.

She smirked at him and tipped her head sideways, so that her neck was exposed. 'Easy enough to find out,' she said to him in a low voice. 'Is that what you want?'

He looked at the smooth skin of her neck. There was no sign of the wound that Lenny had

123

inflicted – they must heal quickly, he supposed. He wanted to touch the skin, see if it really was that smooth.

She laughed at the look on his face. And then her expression changed and, slowly, her upper lip slid back from her teeth. They were neat, small teeth, like a row of pearls across the front. Her canines were longer, but not the dagger-like fangs you see in the movies.

'It's easy,' she said. And then she tossed her head, laughing at the expression of horror on his face.

'That's not what you meant, is it?' she said a short time later, struggling to look serious. She paused, then said, 'It's good for you. That's what they always tell you. It spreads immunity around, protects us from diseases. And anyway,' she concluded, grinning, 'it tastes great!'

More quietly, she added, 'In any case, what I don't really understand is what it's like *without* it. You . . . your kind . . . *creepy*.' She laughed and ran a hand through her spiky hair. 'Who'd have thought?' she said. 'A real live feral. You've got a nerve, haven't you? Marching around as if you own the place. Sneaking up on people in the woods. Who'd have thought?'

He left her a short time later. He had to meet the others. 'I come out here a lot,' she said as he was leaving. 'This is my favourite place.'

He nodded and headed off into the woods.

When he looked back he saw her staring after him. He walked on, not sure if she could still see him in the shade.

It was a mistake, he knew. It could only cause trouble. He remembered his determination earlier that morning to do as Zeb urged him and try to earn the trust of the woodlanders. Talking to Rachel was hardly the best way to do that! But . . . she was fun and she was interested in him and he didn't feel that she was out to trap him with everything she said.

He shook himself, trying to see sense. He forced that image into his head: Rachel, her bloody neck exposed, Lenny and Stacker with her blood smeared across their grinning faces. He didn't know what to think any more. He couldn't get a grip on the rules of this strange and frightening world.

A little later, he met up with Zeb and Rose-Marie. 'Hey,' said Zeb. 'Anything happen?'

Ben shook his head. No. He'd only spent half an hour talking with a vampire who was more human than a lot of the people who lived in the woodland community. That was all.

The Trade

It was dark. Ben had been asleep, but now he was alert.

What had woken him?

He raised himself on his elbows and looked around. The two brothers, Rick and Adam, were asleep a little further along the community hall. At the far end Marty and Jude and their two children were fast asleep. Everyone else lived in the smaller family shelters during the summer months.

Must have been a dream.

He settled himself again. Then he heard footsteps outside, and then the cry again – an animal cry, but Ben knew it was no animal making that sound. It was an alarm call used by woodlanders on lookout duty. There were beasts about.

127

The others were awake now. Ben rose to his feet and moved across to join the brothers. At the far end of the hall, Marty and Jude were calming their children, keeping them silent. Nobody said a word. They were well drilled – at the first sign of trouble, they were to be quiet and stay hidden wherever they were. The community clearing was well hidden from passing paths and trails. Zeb had told him it was four years since a beast had walked through, and even then the signs of settlement had been well hidden. But they were prepared, even so. If the alarm call became higher-pitched and repeated, it meant the beasts were close. If that should happen, the wood-landers would slip away into the surrounding trees, following any of several well-rehearsed routes to safety.

The cry sounded again. A single call – the beasts were near, but were not a serious threat just yet.

Adam had opened the hall's main door a short way. Ben went across to look out into the darkness. There was nothing to see. Whoever had been moving about outside was out of sight now.

The cry again.

Was this the attack that Walter feared? Had the beasts had enough of the foraging raids and decided to round up the ferals? Why else would they be out in the woods in the middle of the night?

Ben waited, his eyes straining against the night's murk.

Nothing.

Then the call changed: lower and softer now. The beasts had passed by. They were a safe distance away.

Ben felt the tension rushing out of his body. He had been holding his breath. Rick and Adam returned to their sleeping area as if this was nothing out of the ordinary. Ben stayed by the door.

He still wasn't used to this life. He had thought he was learning to adapt. Either that or he was relearning the ways of feral life, recovering some of the memories he had blocked out. But the fear was always there, the constant threat from the beasts.

He spotted a small group entering the clearing from one of the woodland trails. Alik was one of them, his long black hair and thick beard distinctive even in the darkness. Robby was there too, strutting along at Alik's side. And just behind them was the taller figure of Zeb, along with two others.

They must have been out foraging, Ben supposed. Raiding a farm or maybe one of the villages or even Kirby itself. He wondered how close they had come to the beasts. He could imagine what it must have been like, hiding out in the woods until the lookout signalled the all-clear. It had been frightening enough for Ben, but to actually have been out in the woods when the alarm went up . . . !

He went back to his sleeping area and tried to shut those thoughts out of his mind. That was the only way, he realized – the only way to live with constant fear is to block it out whenever you can.

Zeb looked as if he'd been in a fight.

The next morning he led Ben and some of the others out to work on what they called 'the barricades' – the woodlanders had constructed a buffer zone surrounding the community clearing.

Over the years, young trees had been trained to grow across any possible paths, and branches had been pulled down to grow across openings. Brambles and honeysuckle had been planted and woven through gaps.

The result was that the area surrounding the settlement was so overgrown that any casual walker would turn away. Only the woodlanders knew the safe paths through the tangled masses of vegetation.

Zeb was quiet as they headed for an area where the barricade was being spread outwards. There were dark shadows under his eyes and his lower lip was cracked and puffed up as if someone had hit him.

After a while, Ben found himself working alongside Zeb, hauling a fallen branch across a space between two trees. They could train honeysuckle over the branch – the cuttings took easily in the rich woodland soil.

'It must have been close last night,' said Ben. 'What happened?'

Zeb looked away. 'Nothing to worry about,' he said.

Ben laughed. 'I'd have been worried if I was you, all right,' he said. 'I heard the alarm calls from the lookouts.'

Zeb shrugged. 'We hid. It was OK.'

Ben pointed at Zeb's face. 'What happened?'

Zeb fingered his cracked lip. 'Shifting livestock,' he said. 'Got a bit lively, that's all.' He turned away.

'You were rustling?' said Ben. 'You mean you actually rustle their animals?'

Zeb glowered at him. 'There's a trade,' he said. 'There's a family who take any stock we can shift. They help protect all this in return for a few favours.'

Ben knew that when he said family he meant a family of beasts . . . He wanted to find out more, but Zeb was moving away from him, over to where Anna was tying brambles in place with twists of sedge.

Ben stared at his retreating back. He hated times like this. Times when he was reminded of how little he really understood about this place and how little the woodlanders trusted him. Zeb was his closest friend in the woodland community, so why did he sometimes treat him like this? Sometimes he thought he would never be accepted here, no matter how hard he tried.

When Zeb slipped away from the group working on the barricade, Ben decided to follow. He was still puzzled by his friend's hostility that morning. Maybe he would be more relaxed away from the others.

Ben had learned his lessons well. Moving silently, and always in the cover of the trees, he followed Zeb for some distance along the trail that led north from the encampment. After a time, he caught up and stepped into the open.

Zeb looked furious, but also he looked uncertain.

'I'll come with you,' said Ben. 'I can help.'

Zeb glanced up at the sun. It was near its highest point – it was almost noon.

'I won't cause any trouble.'

Zeb grunted. 'You're a good kid, Ben,' he said, finally. 'But you *are* trouble . . .' He turned and continued on his way. Ben took that as acceptance and walked at his side.

'You pull stunts like this and you won't last long out here, Ben. Sneak up on Robby or Alik and they'd just slice you. They wouldn't give you a chance to explain yourself.'

'I know,' said Ben. He'd learned more than Zeb gave him credit for. 'I just want to fit in. I want to understand how things work here.'

They followed a narrow trail through the trees.

'Where are you going?' Ben asked a short time later.

'Business,' said Zeb.

They walked, mostly in silence. Finally, they came to a point where the trees thinned and Ben could see a building up ahead. A farmhouse, he guessed.

'The Felson family,' said Zeb. 'Now listen. You wait out in the woods while I go in. Tom Felson is expecting just me. He owes us for last night. I won't be in there long.'

Ben nodded. He knew better than to interfere at this stage.

They came to the last of the trees and Ben stopped. There was a small paddock just ahead of them, then a cluster of low outbuildings, perhaps containing the livestock Zeb and the others had rustled last night.

Tom Felson surprised them, or rather, his dog did.

Just as Zeb set out from the trees, a bundle of black and white fur shot out from nearby and squatted low on its front paws, teeth bared, growling at the two woodlanders.

'Enough,' said a sharp, low voice. 'Lay to.'

The dog settled back on its haunches and stopped growling just as an old man stepped out into the open. He was about Ben's height, with thin grey hair and blue denim dungarees buckled over his shoulders. He leaned on a big staff and peered at his two visitors. He nodded at Zeb, then pointed with his chin towards Ben. 'A new 'un,' he said. 'You bringing presents for me?' He let his upper lip roll back to reveal discoloured teeth and chuckled.

'You have the goods for us?' asked Zeb.

Felson nodded and turned towards the farmhouse. 'Come on.'

Out in the middle of the paddock, Ben felt horribly exposed.

The farmyard was littered with all kinds of debris: barrels, plastic sacks, bits of farm machinery, stacks of tyres, wooden crates. A ginger cat darted across their path, a rat's tail dangling from its mouth. Instantly, the dog gave chase and the old man started to grumble and curse at the animals.

They waited in the yard as the farmer disappeared into the house, re-emerging seconds later with a sports bag. Zeb took the bag and peered inside.

'We asked for a handgun,' he said, glancing at Ben.

Felson shrugged. 'You're not exactly in the strongest bargaining position, are you?'

'You're doing well out of us.'

'You're not doing bad either. There's medicines and drink in there, and there's more where they come from. And there's protection too. Ed McDonnell is getting antsy, but the families won't back him while we're undercutting him and they want to stay in our favour. I'd say you're doing pretty well out of this deal. Just don't go stirring McDonnell up any more, OK?'

'I'll let Alik know what you've told me,' said Zeb. 'He'll want to talk.'

Felson spat on the ground. 'Talk's free,' he said. 'You want to stick around a while?'

Zeb ignored him and headed out of the farmyard, Ben following close on his heels. Every so often he glanced over his shoulder and he could see Tom Felson standing, watching, grinning. He knew exactly what the farmer had wanted when he asked them to stick around for a while.

Memories

She was there again, that afternoon.

Zeb and Rose-Marie had gone off gathering herbs, leaving Ben free to roam for a couple of hours. So he wandered to the clearing where he had spoken with Rachel the day before, and there she was again.

He stayed in the trees for a few minutes, watching her. He should leave now. It would be foolish to do anything else.

She sat on the fallen tree, one foot up on the trunk, her cheek pressed against her raised knee. She had a penknife with a tiny magnifying glass attachment, and she was idly burning charred marks on to the exposed, dead wood. Her pony was tied up nearby.

She looked up and saw him.

He stepped out into the open, feeling guilty.

'I knew you'd be back, Piggy,' she said. 'I can see right through you.'

He walked over and leaned against the fallen tree. 'I was just . . .' He stopped. She was staring at him, smirking.

Finally, she said, 'My old man'd go mad if he knew I was out here talking to a feral. He thinks you should all be rounded up.' She made a pistol shape with her hand and lined it up so that she could stare down her forefinger at Ben. She made a loud explosive sound and laughed. 'He'd go mad,' she said again. 'Mad.'

'And what do *you* think should be done with us?' asked Ben. 'Do you think we should be rounded up too?'

'Of course I do, Piggy. That's why I'm here, isn't it? That's why I'm talking to you. Don't look now, it's a trap! You're surrounded.' She was laughing again. She seemed to spend all her time winding people up. Digging deep, teasing.

'I saw you looking,' she said. 'Earlier. Hiding in the trees. Making sure I was alone.'

'Do you blame me? I've been caught once. I'm not going back.'

'Caught? Who by?'

So he told her some of what had happened after he had first met her in Kirby – feast night, the policeman, Doctor Macreedie.

'Pure of Blood,' she repeated when he told her about the tattooed skinhead. 'That's one of the Purity League's slogans. My father's high up in the League, although he doesn't usually have much to do with skinheads. Keep the blood lines pure, and all that. I wonder what Dad would do if he met someone with it tattooed across his forehead like that?' She giggled at the thought.

'What were you doing in Kirby?' she asked then. 'Why were you lost?'

He looked at her, trying to read her face, trying to work out if he was just going to make a fool of himself yet again.

'I don't know,' he said. 'I can't remember.'

'You never did say where you were from, did you, Piggy? All you said was that you'd been here a couple of weeks.'

He stayed silent.

140

'So where *are* you from?'

'I've told you,' said Ben. 'I don't know.'

'Lost your memory, have you? Or don't you trust me?'

He told her about that afternoon; the walk back across Barlow's Patch, the storm that wasn't a storm, the town that was no longer the town he knew.

'What was your world like before then?' she asked. 'What was so different about it?'

'I don't know,' he said again. He really didn't know what he believed any more. 'What I remember is a world just like this, except there aren't any ... any people like you. A world full of ferals. Maybe there are lots of worlds, different in subtle ways.' He struggled to find the right words for such a big idea. 'Doctor Macreedie told me that ... being like me, being a feral ... was some kind of disease. Maybe it's just different in my world. Whatever it is that made people here need to share blood never happened in my world. And in this world people started drinking blood – or *some* did. Evolution taking a different path. Maybe there are worlds where people are different in some other way.'

He remembered Old Harold demonstrating the idea with the fingers of each hand interlocked. Different worlds pressed close together, sometimes touching . . .

He looked at Rachel. For once she was serious, waiting for him to go on. She was hanging on his words, like the woodland children – stories of other worlds.

He shook his head. 'It seems hard to believe. Even *I'm* having trouble believing it now. All the memories are jumbling up so that I'm not really sure what to believe. Maybe it's all a figment of my imagination, some strange kind of daydream. Maybe this is the only world.'

He paused, then went on. 'Someone told me that this kind of thing has happened to other people. Something bad happens and you block out your memories and replace them with how you'd *like* the world to be, replacing your memories with fantasy. Maybe that's what's happened to me.'

'And you believe that, do you? You think you've lost your memory?'

He shrugged.

'I know what you're going to say,' she interrupted. '"I don't know" – right?'

He smiled, nodded. She knew him so well. 'The more I try to remember my past, the less clear it becomes. It all seems so far away. What would you believe, Rachel? Do you find it easier to believe that I've blocked out some disturbing memories with something much nicer, or that I really have been transported from one world into another?'

'They both sound pretty dumb to me,' she said lightly. 'You might just be a very dull boy who's trying to impress me with big stories, of course. Now, of the three, I'd find that option far easier to believe.'

She leaned towards him, her intense look cutting off his protests. She was so close he could feel her breath on his face.

'But what I do know, Piggy my boy, is that you're the only one who can work it all out. If you're telling stories, then that's fine; I'm used to people lying to me, it happens all the time. But if it's one of the first two options, then only you can tell. You're the one who's been through it, whatever *it* is. You need to trust your own judgement, Piggy. You don't want to rely on other people when it's as important as that.'

The time talking with Rachel seemed to fly past. She was annoying and arrogant, but there was something terribly straightforward about her too. Talking to her seemed to make things clearer somehow.

Talking to her left him more confused too. Confused at his own reactions. She was a *vampire* and yet . . . that moment when she had leaned so close that he could feel her breath on his face . . . it would have been so easy to kiss her. The thought was startling. It excited him and it scared him too.

Most of all though, talking to Rachel was a big mistake – bigger than he realized at the time.

Ben left her by the fallen tree as she prepared to mount her pony and return home. A short distance along the path that led to the top lake, Zeb stepped out in front of him, then Rose-Marie a few paces behind him.

The look on Zeb's face told Ben everything.

'I . . .' started Ben.

Zeb stepped forward and seized him by the wrist, turning him, twisting his arm up painfully behind him.

'We saw you,' said Rose-Marie. 'With the beast. What do you think you were *doing*?' She sounded close to tears. Scared, even. Ben could understand Zeb's anger, but not Rose-Marie's reaction.

'We were only talking,' he said. 'I didn't tell her anything impo–' His words were cut off as Zeb jerked his arm. Ben gasped.

Zeb pushed him forward, still holding his wrist high up behind his back. Ben had to walk, and every step back to the settlement sent a sharp stab of pain through his arm.

'We were only talking,' Ben said again. He was standing in the clearing, the focus of a small, angry group of woodlanders.

His tormentor, Alik, was walking in front of him, back and forth, his eyes never leaving Ben's face. He was carrying a knife with a blade the length of his forearm. One of the onlookers, Robby, had already told anyone who would listen that they should split Ben open from chin to balls and leave him for the crows to peck at.

Walter had put a stop to that, but even he had stopped short of defending Ben. Now he stood back with Zeb in the crowd, letting Alik run whatever kind of trial this was.

'*Only talking*,' Alik said. He liked to repeat what Ben said, using his words to make him look guilty. 'You and a beast . . . *only talking.*'

'I didn't give anything away,' said Ben in a low voice. He looked at Zeb and Rose-Marie, but they turned away. No one was willing to give him a chance. 'I just want to understand what this world is like – how it works.'

'You want to understand,' said Alik, pausing briefly in his pacing. 'Let me tell you how it *doesn't* work, OK? It doesn't work by just anyone deciding to talk to the beasts. It doesn't work by newcomers deciding to endanger the entire community just to satisfy their own stupid curiosity. OK?'

'*You* talk to them,' said Ben accusingly. 'You talk to Tom Felson.'

That made Alik falter for a moment. Then he said, 'Of course. On behalf of the community. Felson's useful to have on our side. We have to trade in order to survive, but we do it selectively. We do it very carefully. Our lives depend on it. We don't just go and chat with them because we feel like it!'

'She's different.' Sometimes Ben was too stubborn for his own good. He should stay quiet. He shouldn't provoke Alik, shouldn't encourage the vengeful thoughts of Robby and his like.

'*Different*,' repeated Alik. 'There's no such thing as *different* where the beasts are concerned. They're all the same.' He caught Walter's eye and nodded.

Walter stepped forward now. 'He's right,' he explained. 'It's the sharing, the mixing of blood. Do you understand why they do it, Ben?'

'They share immunity to diseases,' said Ben, remembering what Rachel had told him.

Walter nodded. 'Yes, but that's only part of it. Every time a beast drinks another one's blood, it picks up traces of memories carried in the blood. It's a chemical thing, a kind of collective consciousness. Some of them have memories going back generations. They're not individuals like we are, Ben. They're like bees in a beehive. That girl isn't any different to the others, no matter *what* she claims. Her head is full of the thoughts and memories of her parents and brothers and uncles and whoever else she's shared with.'

'But what about the ones you trade with?'

'That's different,' said Walter. 'Blood-sharing is a family thing – the beasts share blood with each other far more than they do with outsiders. We're careful about which families we deal with and they're careful to guard their business secrets.'

Ben remembered Doctor Macreedie's disapproval of blood-sharing taking place outside the family. He remembered Macreedie's toddler drinking greedily at its mother's neck. And he remembered Rachel saying how her father would have the ferals rounded up if he could.

Her father! If blood-sharing was a family thing then he would drink her blood – and he would taste her memories . . . memories of Ben, of talking in the woods with a feral. Her father would be after them then, for sure. Now, suddenly, Ben understood Rose-Marie's fear, and he understood all the anger and hostility. He'd betrayed them, put them all at risk. He hadn't meant to, he hadn't understood, but still he had betrayed them all.

'Every feast day they share blood,' said Walter. 'And then they will all know everything she knows.'

Ben remembered Rachel staring down her forefinger at him, her hand in the shape of a pistol. How could he ever have trusted her? He looked at Walter, at Alik and the watching crowd.

'What are we going to do with him?' asked Robby from nearby.

Alik raised his long knife and stared at the blade, as if checking the steel for flaws. 'Nothing,' he said softly, unexpectedly. 'We do nothing, for now.'

'What?' Robby was pink with anger.

Alik silenced him with a chopping motion of

his hand through the air. Then he stepped over to Ben and placed a hand on his shoulder. His fingers toyed with the fabric of Ben's shirt.

'You know what you've got to do, don't you?' he hissed.

Ben stared at him. 'What?'

'You've got to meet her again before the next feast day. Some time in the next eight days. Before she's shared her blood with her family. You've got to convince her that you've only ever been on your own here in the woods and then you tell her you're moving on. Some place far, far away.'

'Make her believe you,' said Walter. 'Because if you don't, then next feast day they'll be all over the woods looking for you.'

'And finding all of *us*,' finished Alik.

Ben swallowed. 'And then . . . ?'

Alik stepped back, slid his knife into a sheath. 'And then we decide what to do with *you*.'

The Farmer's Daughter

The next day it rained heavily and Ben knew she wouldn't be there. He went to the clearing, even so. It got him away from the menacing looks and whispers.

It was good to get away from them all. They had never trusted him, and now he had made it all so much worse.

The clearing seemed strange without Rachel and her pony. Ben went to sit on the fallen tree and instantly the dampness started to soak through his jeans. He stayed there for a long time, but she didn't show up.

Walter was waiting for him where the path cut through the barricade, fussing over newly planted honeysuckle.

'I'm sorry,' he said softly.

Ben peered at him, puzzled by this change in attitude.

'You really didn't understand, did you? It never occurred to us that you might talk to them, but then it never occurred to us that you didn't appreciate the risks involved. There seem to be so many gaps in your memory.'

'I'm not from here,' said Ben.

'So you say.'

He remembered Old Harold's explanation – worlds so similar and yet so different. Worlds so close, like the interlocking fingers of two hands. Somehow he had crossed from one hand to the other. If there were two worlds so close, there could be many more, each slightly different from the others. It was a daunting thought.

'The girl's father will come after us if he knows she's talked to you. He'll be outraged. He'll think she's at risk – his daughter mixing with the wild folk!

'Some of the beasts are OK – or, at least, we can deal with them and they leave us in peace. But McDonnell is different. He's obsessed with the idea of purity – keeping the bloodlines separate. Arranged marriages, keeping the families pure, no mixing of races. If he knows his daughter has made friends with one of *us* . . .'

'She mentioned the Purity League,' Ben said. 'Some group her father belongs to.'

'They're fascists,' said Walter. 'Racial fanatics. The man is an extremist, and, what's more, he's a powerful extremist. From what we hear, McDonnell has been wanting to hunt us down for ages, but he can't do it alone. He needs the support of his neighbours. Maybe he'd be able to use this to win some of them over. Ferals getting close to their children – that would scare some of them, all right.'

'What's wrong with us being different?' said Ben. 'Why shouldn't we be able to live our lives out here?'

'You may well ask,' said Walter. 'To people like McDonnell we're just *too* different. Our kind have their place and it's not out here in the wild. He'd have us rounded up, treated like animals, or worse. McDonnell and his friends wouldn't even accept that we're basically the same species.

Blood-sharing goes back a long time in human history, but we all started out the same.'

'Doctor Macreedie said our resistance to sharing is like a disease – some kind of flaw in our genes.'

Walter shook his head. 'It's the other way round, Ben. People like McDonnell don't like to admit it, but back in history there was a time when there were no beasts. Blood-sharing was an abomination that hardly anyone practised. But then it spread like some kind of disease. That's the best description I can come up with – a plague, passed from one person to another. And, as with any disease, some are immune to it. Through history our numbers have steadily fallen. Now, as far as we can tell, there are only isolated groups scattered through Europe, holding out where we can. The fascist purity leagues would wipe us out like vermin if they could.'

'In my world,' said Ben, 'there was no plague of blood-sharing. That's where the difference is.'

'Whatever,' said Walter, clearly disappointed that Ben was still sticking to his story. 'To an extremist like McDonnell, the resistant population are a freak of nature. We don't fit into his neat view of how the world should be and so he'd think nothing of wiping us out just to tidy things up a bit.'

The next day was brighter, and there was a freshness about the vegetation that had been missing in the dry spell before the rain. Everything was coming back to life. It seemed like a good sign and suddenly Ben felt optimistic.

In the afternoon he went to the clearing and waited but, again, Rachel didn't turn up. Was it the end of the school holidays already? he wondered. He had completely lost track of the passing days. He sat on the fallen tree and tried to work it out. After a few minutes, he decided that it was still only late August. So where was she?

Perhaps they had shared blood already ... Perhaps they had tasted her memories and knew that she had been meeting a wild boy in the woods.

According to Rose-Marie there was still a week to go until the next feast day, but was she really sure? Ben remembered Rachel sharing blood with her two friends, Lenny and Stacker. Maybe that was how their secret had slipped out . . .

He left the clearing. On the west side there was a wide trail through the woods that Rachel called the Foxglove Ride. Ben knew that was the way she came from Tippham.

He set off along the ride.

He wasn't going to do anything foolish, he was just going for a look. He could hide at the edge of the woods and look across the fields towards the farm. Maybe he would see her. Maybe he could attract her attention.

This was the way they had come on the night they had finally trusted him enough to take him on a farm raid – along the Foxglove Ride and then across the fields to the farm. He remembered the journey back, helping Zeb with the tools they had taken from the barn. He wondered if they would ever trust him even that much again. It had seemed so much farther in the darkness. Now, after about half an hour, he was approaching the woodland edge.

He saw her straight away. She was on her grey pony, trotting along the track that cut across a field towards the woods. He should have been more patient. He should have waited for her. For a moment he considered retreating to the trees and cutting back to their usual meeting place. But that would take another half hour and she might not still be there by the time he arrived.

He stood at the edge of the ride, waiting in the shade of the trees.

'Piggy!' she said, a short time later. 'What are you doing out here?'

'I came looking for you,' he said. 'I wanted to see you, to talk.'

'Sounds serious,' she said with mock solemnity. She jumped down from the pony's back. 'Tell me more.'

'I'm moving on,' he said. 'I'm going.' He remembered their talks in the woods. He had felt trusted, but all the time she had been betraying him – betraying him with the memory traces carried in her blood.

'Going?' she said, losing her usual confident tone. 'Where? Why?'

'I don't know,' he said. 'I'll head south, I reckon. I came to the woods because I'd heard that there might be others like me here, but I was wrong. I have to keep looking. I can't live on my own in the woods forever.'

For a moment he thought she believed him. Just for a moment. And then he saw the look on her face – puzzled, hurt, angry.

'What's changed, Piggy? Why are you lying to me?'

'It's true,' he said. 'I'm going.' He had to keep it up. He had to convince her somehow.

'You haven't been living alone, Piggy. I know that. Oh, you've been careful, all right. You haven't told me where you live or how many of you there are, but you're not on your own here, Piggy. And if you're lying about that, you're probably lying about leaving too. So what's happened to make you start lying to me?'

'You didn't tell me the truth,' said Ben. 'I asked you why your kind share blood and you only told me about sharing immunity. And the taste.'

They were standing toe to toe, so close that Ben could see the restless twitching of Rachel's upper lip, the pearly top row of teeth it concealed.

'You didn't tell me about the memories,' he went on. 'You didn't tell me that when you share blood you share memories too. You tell me that your father would have people like me rounded up if he knew we were here. You claim that you're not like him. But all the time, you have his blood in your veins. His memories. You must think like him in some ways too, mustn't you? All this time it amuses you to come to the woods and talk to a feral, but I bet you still think we should be rounded up – that we shouldn't be living here at all!'

'That's what you think, is it?' There were tears welling in her eyes, angry tears. 'I'm not my father. I *am* different. So your wild friends have been telling you that we're all the same, have they?

'It doesn't work like that. Yes, we share memories. I can close my eyes and remember exactly what it was like to fight in the trenches in the Great War – Great Grandad was there. He made sure those memories were passed on so that we would all know how awful it was. But there are other memories that you don't want to pass on. You can block it out, Piggy. You can learn to control the way memories imprint on your blood.

'Do you really think I'm just like my father? Do you think I'd come out here and meet you if that was true? Or is it really that you're scared I'll give you away? Is that it?'

Ben shrugged. He felt horribly guilty. He didn't know who to believe. Rachel and Zeb were the only friends he had made in this mad world. Was this really *her* talking to him? Or was it the part of her that was her father, struggling to persuade him that it was OK to confide in her . . . ?

'I don't know,' he said. He never seemed to know.

'Let me show you,' she said suddenly. She reached for his hand and took it in hers. Her touch was warm. Somehow he had expected it to be cold, like that of a corpse.

'What do you mean?'

'Come back to the farm with me and I'll show you exactly why you should trust me. Come on, Piggy. Let me prove it to you.'

'But . . .'

'Come on, Piggy. Just a quick look. It'll be OK. We won't see anyone, and if we do I'll just tell them you're a new boy from Kirby.'

It was his best chance to convince her, he realized. If he went with her, then he would be in her confidence again and so, when he insisted that he was moving on, maybe she would believe him. He remembered how long it had taken Doctor Macreedie to be sure he was a feral. Surely he would be able to carry off a short visit to the farm without being found out? Maybe by taking a risk like this he would convince the woodlanders that they could rely on him to do the right thing.

'OK,' he said. 'But I *am* moving on. I can't stay around here.' And perhaps that was true, after all. Perhaps he would leave the community and try to find somewhere better.

But first, he had to go to the farm with Rachel.

They rode there on the pony.

'It's OK,' said Rachel, leaning down to help Ben up behind her. 'Champion's strong enough to carry the two of us.'

She sat forward in the saddle and there was

just enough room for Ben to sit behind her, his arms around her waist. Sitting like this, her neck was centimetres from his face, and he could see that her skin wasn't as flawless as he had thought. Its smoothness was punctuated by the neat white indentations where others had feasted. Some of the marks looked fresh.

She turned and smiled, deliberately baring her teeth. She smiled more broadly when she saw the startled look pass over his features. 'I won't bite,' she said. 'I promise.'

He closed his eyes and concentrated on holding on tight, enjoying being so close to this maddening, exciting girl.

They emerged from the woods and headed along the track that cut through the fields to Tippham. No turning back now. To either side, the fields were golden with barley, ready for the harvest. Over Rachel's shoulder, Ben could see the silhouettes of the farm buildings up ahead. The farmhouse itself was a solid red-brick build-ing, and was surrounded by big square-edged barns and a succession of the long, semi-circular livestock buildings like the community hall back in the woods. He remembered Zeb saying that they kept mainly pigs and cattle on this farm. He wondered what it was that Rachel was going to show him.

They crossed the farmyard and rounded the corner of one of the barns. And there was a young man standing there, brushing down one of the other horses.

'Hi, Pete,' said Rachel casually as they rode past.

He looked up and grunted.

When they were out of earshot, Rachel reached down to squeeze Ben's knee and whispered, 'It's OK. Pete looks after the horses. He didn't notice a thing.'

A few seconds later they stopped. 'Go on then,' said Rachel. 'You have to get off first.'

Reluctantly, Ben eased his grip on her waist. He swung his leg over the horse, then realized too late that he didn't have anywhere to put his foot and tumbled in a heap on the ground.

Rachel sat back in the saddle, giggling. 'Don't they have horses where you come from, Piggy?' she asked him.

He clambered to his feet and brushed himself down. He felt angry with her, but suddenly he understood that she was the one in control now – he was on her territory, he was relying on her completely. Why had he come here?

She jumped down from the saddle and led the pony into the stables. 'We'll leave him saddled,' she said, as she shut the half-door on the horse. 'We can ride back into the woods in a few minutes.'

She looked sideways at him and hesitated.

'So?' said Ben. 'What is it? What have you brought me here to see?'

She took his hand and led him along one side of the stable block. At the end there was another small yard and on the far side the semi-circular end wall of one of the livestock buildings.

They crossed the yard.

There was a door set into the wall, but they didn't go there. Instead, Rachel led him to a row of windows, set head-high in the wall.

As they approached, Ben heard the animal grunts he remembered from the night of the raid. 'What's in there?' he asked Rachel. 'What is it?'

'Pigs,' she said in a low voice. 'Daddy's a pig farmer.'

Ben looked through the first of the windows into the piggery. It was gloomy inside and the glass was filthy and smeared. It took a moment for his eyes to adjust and then, with a sudden shock, Ben understood why Rachel called him 'Piggy'.

'This is a specialist farm,' she explained. 'We keep them for the blood. It's sold in supermarkets as a luxury product. They have dull minds, but their blood is always in demand. There's a lot of money to be made in pigs' blood.'

Ghostly figures, pressed tight together in the gloom. Pale faces, turned towards the light of the row of windows. Perhaps they could see Ben's head silhouetted against the window as he looked in at them. The creatures were naked and filthy and constantly on the move. Walking in tight circles, bumping and jostling each other, and grunting like pigs. Except . . . they were not pigs.

'You see?' said Rachel. 'My father thinks all the ferals should be rounded up and kept in a piggery like this. That's your race's position in the world – all you're fit for. If I was just like my father, I'd believe that too. Do you really think I'm like that? Do you really think I'd want you kept in a piggery like this? It's *horrible* . . . cruel.'

Ben backed away from the window. He breathed deeply, trying to calm himself. They were monsters, keeping people in factory farms like this. Beasts – the ferals' name for the vampires was an appropriate one. He looked at Rachel.

'Do you trust me now?' she asked.

He nodded. He had to get out of this awful place. He had to get back to the woods.

'All right then,' she said. 'I'm sorry, Piggy. But I had to show you this so you could see that I'm on your side. Let's go back to the woods.'

'Rachel, darling. And who's this?'

There was a tall woman standing across the small yard. She smiled at them, and her piercing eyes were fixed on Ben's face.

'Oh, hi, Mum. This is Ben,' said Rachel, slipping instantly into her cocky, confident mode. 'The new boy in my class. I told you about him, didn't I? He moved into Kirby about a month ago.'

Rachel's mother looked blank. 'I don't *think* you mentioned him,' she said hesitantly.

'Course I did,' said Rachel. 'He goes round with Stacker and Lenny and me sometimes. Come on, Ben. I said I'd show him the woods. He's a birdwatcher.'

Rachel set off across the yard and Ben followed. And all the time, Rachel's mother watched him. It reminded him of the staring faces in Kirby. Maybe it was just his imagination.

Rachel's mother stepped into their path. 'It's teatime, darling,' she said. 'Come in and have something to eat and then you can go out for a short time afterwards.'

'We'll have something later,' said Rachel. 'Come on, P– Ben. Let's get Champion.'

But Ben stopped. He had heard footsteps behind him. He looked over his shoulder and Pete, the stable hand, was standing a short distance away, a pitchfork in one hand. He was staring at Ben, just as Rachel's mother had been staring at him. Eyes never leaving his face.

Rachel turned. She saw Pete. 'What is it?' she said hesitantly. Then, 'Come on, Ben. Let's go.'

'No, Rachel. You're not going out again this evening.' This time it was a man's voice. The middle-aged man Ben had seen on the night of the raid. Rachel's father. He was standing by his wife's side now, a shotgun held at waist height.

'Go to your room, Rachel,' the man said. 'This isn't your business any more. I'll talk to you later. After I've dealt with this wild pig.'

The Farmer

Rachel stood rooted to the spot, staring at her father.

Nobody moved for a few seconds, then her mother stepped forward, took her by the arm and led her silently away. At the door, Rachel paused, resisting her mother's pressure, and looked back at Ben. The tears were streaming down her face now.

She went inside.

Her father was a well-built man, broad-shouldered, with a belly that spilled over the top of his belted trousers. His face was thin though, his cheeks hollowed so that his eyes appeared to bulge.

He moved closer, stopping a short distance in front of Ben. He still held the gun at waist height, and now it was pointing somewhere about Ben's midriff.

'You're one of the bright ones, aren't you?' he said in a rumbling, deep voice. 'One of the ones that can talk. You understand me, don't you? You've been talking to Rachel, after all. Giving her strange ideas.'

He licked his lips. 'Strange ideas, yes. She thought she could stop us from finding out, but I could taste the guilt on her. I could taste the strange piggish ideas in her blood. Wild pig. We kept her in for a while, to stop her from seeing you. But then I thought, let's trap you. Let's use you.

'You're going to talk, pig. You're going to talk to us and tell us all you know about the wild ones that hide in the woods and raid my farm. You're going to tell us where to find them, aren't you, pig?'

The man's eyes were bulging even more now. He was leaning forward, his face close enough to Ben's that he could smell the beast's fetid breath.

'You know what we do to wild pigs, do you?' He pushed the barrel of the gun into Ben's belly.

'We round them up and put them in the piggeries where they belong.'

Then he laughed.

'But we don't want them spreading foolish ideas.' He took Ben's face in one big hand. 'So we cut out their tongues,' he said. 'Stop them talking. And if they cause trouble we cut off their balls too. Do you hear what I'm saying, pig? Do . . . you . . . understand . . . what . . . I'm . . . saying?'

The stable hand, Pete, grabbed Ben's arms from behind. Rachel's father turned and marched into the house and Pete forced Ben to follow.

The kitchen was full of pine furniture, the wood turned a rich golden colour over the years. A dead bird – a chicken or a duck, or maybe a pheasant – lay on a chopping board, its feathers plucked, its belly split open and its insides exposed to the world. Washing hung to dry on a wooden rack suspended from the high ceiling.

They sat him at the kitchen table. Pete took the shotgun while Rachel's father sat opposite Ben.

'Where are the others?' he said.

Ben shook his head.

'Talk, pig.'

'There are no others,' said Ben in a shaky voice. 'I'm on my own.'

'Don't waste my time with lies,' said the farmer. 'Where are they living and how many are there?'

'I've been living rough in the woods,' said Ben. 'A clearing with a fallen tree where Rachel sometimes goes on Champion.'

The farmer leaned forward, his hands spread flat on the table. 'Save yourself,' he demanded. 'Tell me the truth.'

Ben stayed silent.

The two men exchanged a glance. Pete put down the shotgun and took hold of Ben's arms again.

'You can't hide it from us,' said the farmer. 'The truth is in your blood.'

He stood and moved round the table.

Ben struggled against the stable hand's grip, but it was no use. The man was too strong for Ben. He wouldn't let go.

The farmer was close now.

'It's the truth!' said Ben. 'I'm on my own. I don't know what you're talking about.'

The farmer took Ben's jaw in a firm grip and pushed his head back, exposing his throat. Ben tried to turn and twist, but he was held too tight. He tried to empty his mind, to think only of that clearing in the woods where he met Rachel, where they had talked together and where it seemed for a time that he had found a true friend.

But no! That was a mistake. When he thought of Rachel he thought of the smoothness of her skin, the way she moved, the sound of her laugh. He didn't want her father to taste such thoughts in his blood – that would only feed his anger.

He thought instead of the fallen tree. Dark, peeling bark. Almost black. Deeply rutted and warped, so that you could stare at the patterns it made and see shapes that weren't really there. The white wood where the bark had peeled away. Rachel's graffiti, carved with a penknife. Her own name, repeated over and over. Black char marks where she had burned the wood with the small magnifying glass that was part of her penknife.

He felt the hot breath on his exposed neck.

He thought of the broken branch where she tied Champion. The rich green grass that grew in the clearing. The grey pony, head down, eating the grass.

Firm, dry lips, pressing against his neck. The scrape of the farmer's stubbly chin.

He thought of Rachel's tears, that last look she had given him before being shepherded into the farmhouse. She had really believed that she had blocked out her memories, hidden them from her father. He tried to blank his mind, to forget everything.

The teeth.

Two sharp points of pressure on his neck. Hard. Hurting.

The sudden release as his skin broke in two places.

He cried out, but the sound choked off in his throat.

It hurt more than anything he had ever known. Worse than the leg he had broken when he was six. Worse than when he had trodden barefoot on a windfall apple full of wasps when he was a toddler.

Worse than anything.

But only for a few seconds. Then it turned into a dull, fuzzy ache, which spread out from the wounds, wrapping around his neck and across the back of his head. Blackness started to spread across his mind. For a second, he was only aware of the ache, the feeling that his body was being turned inside out like a glove. And then he drifted.

The darkness closed around him.

The Piggery

Animal noises, all around.

Heat.

An overpowering smell of unwashed bodies, urine, faeces.

He felt sick.

And tired.

So tired.

He knew he should open his eyes, but the effort was simply too much for him.

Something was pulling at his clothes. Insistent, animal movements.

He tried to move, but his body didn't respond.

He was lying on a hard surface, lying in something wet.

Something stumbled over him, trod on his left

leg just below the knee. He gasped, but still he couldn't find the energy to move.

He opened his eyes. Peered out through the slitted openings between his eyelids.

Dark shapes moved around. Silhouettes against a series of grey rectangles.

Animals.

No, people.

Pigs.

He was in the piggery. They'd put him in the piggery.

He opened his eyes again. He realized that some time must have passed, but had no idea how long.

The series of grey rectangles must be the windows. They were dimmer now, the interior of the piggery even gloomier. It must be evening then. Or night.

His throat was dry. He tried to swallow, but the dryness made it painful.

He turned his head to one side and instantly pain daggered through his neck.

They'd bitten him. They'd drunk his blood so that they could taste his memories.

Something pulled at him again.

He raised a hand to fend it off.

'It'? All these 'its' were people . . . pigs.

He forced himself up on to his elbows and peered around in the gloom. There was a naked man squatting at Ben's side, pulling at his clothes.

Ben managed to raise a hand again, made a pushing movement at the man.

The man bared his teeth and lunged at Ben's hand, as if he was going to bite.

Ben pulled away, scared.

The sudden movement set his head spinning. It took a long time for the dizziness to ease, and when it did there were two naked children with the man, pulling at Ben's clothes again.

Ben shuffled away from them, struggling to haul his weary body across the wet, muddy floor.

There were people all around. They snarled at him whenever he bumped into them. All around him, the snuffling, grunting sounds were suddenly deafening, overpowering.

He came to a corrugated metal wall. He pressed his back against it, tucked his knees up against his chest. He wrapped his arms around his legs and buried his face. Trying to block it all out. Trying to pretend this wasn't happening.

But there was no escaping the constant animal noises, the penetrating smell of the piggery. He felt sick, but he didn't have the energy to throw up. He barely even had the energy to stay upright.

The blackness wrapped itself around him again.

He woke. More time had passed.

This time he could stand.

'Water,' he gasped to the woman standing pressed against his side. So little space! Like battery hens.

She stared at him, then grunted and reached out a hand to stroke his clothes.

He pushed himself away from her, and instantly a man snarled at him.

He threaded his way through the throng, trying to avoid contact with the pressing bodies wherever possible.

Eventually, he found a metal trough, bolted on to one wall. He couldn't see what it contained, so he dipped a finger into its depths. Liquid. He raised his finger, sniffed, tasted. Just water.

He bent over the trough, scooped up a handful of water and drank. It felt good, easing the pain in his throat a little. He was starting to come back to his senses. He took another handful of water. Another.

He wasn't sure he liked coming back to his senses though. It meant he could think again. Understand. The awful truth of his situation started to sink in. He had been caught and thrown into the piggery, where he belonged.

Two weeks? Three weeks? Was that all it had been? Watching the football with Andy. Afterwards, having a kickabout in the back garden.

And now this.

He tried not to think about the future, about the farmer's threats of what they do to wild ferals to keep them under control.

That was when his body started to shake uncontrollably, when the tears of anger and fear finally broke loose.

*

In the night, he dreamed of quicksand. Quicksand that had a pungent smell: a mixture of urine, decay and the sweaty reek of unwashed bodies.

He woke, and bodies were pressed all around him as he lay on the hard floor of the piggery. They were pressed so tight he could barely move. The smell of the bare flesh against his face repelled him and he wanted to move away, but they pressed against him from all sides.

He drifted back to sleep again, the heavy tiredness in his limbs unlike anything he had felt before.

As dawn's thin light started to spread through the piggery, he woke again. This time he felt strong enough to work himself free of the pressing bodies and sit with his back against the wall.

So many people! He could barely see the straw-covered concrete floor for the mass of slumbering bodies.

He remembered his grandad telling him about a Norfolk broiler house where he had once worked – a great barn with what he described as a carpet of tightly packed chickens. When one died it would get trampled by the others, eventually ending up so flat it had to be peeled from the floor.

Ben put his head in his hands and held it tight, trying to stop the dizziness, the nausea.

Over in the far corner, where the drinking and food troughs were, he saw the dark shapes of rats scurrying about. At one point, one dropped from a ledge and ran across the sleeping bodies to get to the next trough. Ben looked away.

One by one, the people around him woke and stretched and clambered to their feet.

He stood too, feeling vulnerable on the floor with them all looming over him. He pressed against the wall, hoping not to be noticed.

They walked.

That was what these people *did*. With small, shuffling paces, they walked around the piggery, never stopping. It passed the time, he supposed.

He watched them, studying their big, sunken eyes, their shaggy hair, their thin bodies. He wondered how the vampires could treat people like this.

Standing alone, Ben was conspicuous, and soon they were gathering around him again, hands reaching to touch his clothes, faces pressing close from all around, eyes staring.

He tried to shrink away from the rising animal din of grunts and chattering sounds, but his back was to the wall already and there was nowhere for him to go. He put his hands before his face, but immediately they were batted away by a big fist.

'What do you want?' he gasped. 'Will you just please leave me alone?'

Some of them backed away at the sound of his words. Maybe it made them think he was a beast, somehow cast into their midst.

These people – at times they seemed so very different from Ben that he started to see how the vampires might blind themselves to their humanity and treat them as animals. But were they really that different or was it simply that they were treated this way? Treat a person like an animal and they'll behave like one.

It was time he behaved like one too. He started to walk, copying the small steps and slow pace of the others. He felt less exposed now. Those around him stared, and every so often they reached out to touch his clothes, but they seemed less threatening like this.

After some time, he realized that the pace had slowed and the bodies were packing more tightly towards one end of the piggery. There was light! So much brighter than the gloom of the piggery. It flooded in through an open doorway. They were being let out.

Ben wondered if there was some kind of outside exercise area. He stood in the ramshackle queue for what seemed like ages, but eventually he came to the opening. The farmhand, Pete, was there, and two others Ben hadn't seen before. They used short, pointed sticks to split the farmed people into three lines, leading across a short open area and into another barn.

When Ben's turn came, Pete flicked him across the ribs with the side of his stick and said, 'Not you. Back inside, you hear?'

Ben looked at him, confused. Pete hit him again, harder this time, and Ben stepped aside so that those behind him could get through. He took a backward step just as Pete raised his stick again.

'Don't want to bleed you dry, now do we? Don't worry, you'll get to see the milking parlour tomorrow.'

Ben slipped back into the piggery.

The 'milking parlour'.

Rachel's father had sucked Ben's blood the previous evening. It must be too soon to 'milk' him again . . .

Alone in the vast piggery, the awfulness of his situation struck him again.

Ben sat and rested his chin on his knees. He closed his eyes and there was just the smell and the images in his head. He stayed like that for some time and then he realized that he had a choice. He could sit here like this, getting even more gloomy about what had happened or he could try to do something.

He stood. He went first to the doors which led through to the yard and the milking parlour. They were shut firm – probably locked from the outside.

He came to the row of windows. From the

inside they were just above head-height, but it was possible to hang on to the window sills and hold himself so that he could see out across the yard to the stables and the house beyond. The windows were enclosed by a metal grid so that, even if he could unfasten one from the inside, it would only open a short distance.

He dropped back to the ground and continued on his circuit of the piggery. He paused to relieve himself in the trough that was clearly intended for this purpose, backing away from the cloud of flies it stirred up.

There was nothing. There was no way out of this place unless the beasts let you out.

He returned to the windows and pulled himself up to look out. Through a gap in the buildings he saw a car pull up at the house and, a short time later, another. He wondered if this was normal farm activity or if it might be the start of some kind of round-up – Rachel's father calling together his neighbours to take action against the woodland community.

He looked up at the farmhouse and saw a small, pale face in one window. Rachel!

At this distance, and through the smeared glass of the piggery window, he couldn't see much detail, but he *knew* it was Rachel. He wished there was some way he could signal to her, but there was none. He dropped down to the floor and started to pace around the piggery once again.

They came back, shuffling, slow-motion. Like zombies.

Their pale bodies almost glowed in the murky light of the piggery.

Ben realized then that there were no elderly people here. They either died young, he supposed, or were culled when they grew too weak and old.

Pete and the hands dumped hard food-cakes into two of the troughs and Ben worked his way through the passive crowd to take one. It was hard and sweet and he had to gnaw at it to break even a small piece off. It calmed the rumbling in his stomach though.

He carried on walking, looking. Hoping to spot something that might help him get out of this awful place.

*

Had he imagined it? All he could hear now were animal noises all around.

He strained to hear anything different above the din, but there was nothing. His mind playing tricks, that was all.

But the people around him were unsettled, disturbed by something. They had heard it too.

'Piggy!' A girl's voice, faint, almost smothered by the endless grunting and groaning of the farmed humans.

'Piggy!' Louder. It was Rachel.

Ben tried to work out where the call was coming from, but it was impossible. He turned and twisted and a woman lashed out at him, her fist glancing off the side of his head. It was evening now, and the farmed people had recovered from being milked.

'Piggy!'

He pushed through a gap between bodies. Ahead, he could see the grey rectangles of the row of windows. There was a dark shape there. A head and shoulders silhouetted against the faint light that spilled in from the farmyard. The window was open a crack, as far as it would go against a restraining metal grid. She was calling through the gap again.

'Piggy! Are you there?'

She didn't see him, even when he was close to the window.

'Rachel,' he rasped. 'I'm here.'

'Piggy. Oh, Piggy. I'm sorry. I never thought . . . I never meant . . .'

'I know,' he said through the gap. 'You didn't think they knew. You thought you'd blocked out the memories.'

'I didn't mean it to be like this.'

She was crying, Ben thought. 'It's not your fault,' he said.

'Are you OK? My father shut me in my room, but I had to sneak out and see if you were OK.'

Ben looked back across the inside of the piggery. 'I'm OK,' he said. 'I'm sore and I'm weak from the bleeding, but I'm OK. Listen, Rachel, is there any way you can get me out of here?'

She was silent for a long time. Finally, she said, 'I don't know. My father . . .'

It was a big thing he was asking, he realized.

'You were right,' he said. 'There *are* other

ferals in the woods. I lied to you to protect them. I thought that if I could convince you I was alone your father might leave them in peace. But they're all in danger now. They're people, Rachel – just like you and me. We have to help them.'

Silence again.

Then, 'OK, Piggy. I'll get you out. Wait by the main door. I'll be back.'

He moved along to wait for her, wondering if she would return.

Eventually, there was a scraping sound and the door edged outwards.

'Piggy?'

'I'm here.' He slipped out through the gap. Behind him, the others just stared at the opening, making no move to escape.

Rachel closed the door and he leaned on it, struggling to calm himself, breathing the fresh evening air deeply. 'You should let them all out,' he said.

'You saw them,' she said. 'They don't have a clue. They wouldn't know what to do if we turned them out. All they've ever known is the inside of a barn. They're bred for it. Set them loose and any that weren't hunted down inside a couple of hours would just die.'

She was right, he knew. It was all so cruel and wrong, yet what could he do to change it? There must be so many piggeries like this one. What could any one person do?

'They shouldn't be kept like that,' said Ben.

'I know,' she said in a quiet voice. 'I'm sorry, Piggy. Everything's gone wrong and it's all my fault.'

Ben tipped his head back, despite the pain in his neck. He stared at the stars. He didn't know what to say.

'He used me,' Rachel said. 'My father. I don't know how long he's known about you, but he hid it from me so he could use me.'

'Use you to catch me,' said Ben. 'Taste my blood, read my memories so he can find out about the ferals.'

She peered across at him, and he could see that she was crying again. 'You're right,' she said. 'Your friends are in danger. I listened in on Dad this evening. He's been calling the families together so that they can round up the ferals. I heard what's behind all this too. There have been ferals in the woods for years and nobody's ever really been bothered. They raid the farms some-times, and they steal crops from the fields, but they never do much damage. Sometimes one gets caught or shot, and sometimes a few are trapped and we put them in the piggeries to add a bit of variety to the breeding stock. That's just the way things are.'

'So what's different now? Why's your dad so keen to round us up?'

'Someone's been smuggling,' she said. 'Ferals. They've been smuggling and Dad wants to put an end to it.'

'Smuggling what?' But even as he spoke, all the pieces were slotting into place and he knew the terrible answer to his own question. He remembered Zeb telling him about the trade with some of the families. He remembered that night when Zeb had come back with a split lip. They had been rustling, he'd said – the livestock had been hard to handle, had put up a bit of a fight.

People. Was that it? The 'livestock'?

She saw the look of understanding on his face

and nodded. 'They've been smuggling wild pigs . . . people. It started up a few years ago. Undermining the farms with an alternative supply of wild blood. Not much. But any new varieties are worth a lot of money. Nobody knew where it was coming from until you told me your story and Dad read it in my blood. Piggy, someone's worked out how to open a way from other worlds into this one and they've been using it to smuggle people like you through. And now Dad knows the ferals have been dealing with the Felson family! And trying to get guns . . . The families won't allow that to happen.'

The more Ben thought about her words, the more everything fell into place: he must have slipped through their grip. Something must have gone wrong as he was plucked from his own world. Maybe they'd been interrupted, the disturbance allowing him to wander free.

The ferals of the community – he couldn't believe that they all knew what was going on. But Alik . . . He could believe it of Alik. Trading humans for protection. That must be why he was so hostile towards Ben – he had recognized that his story was true and that Ben's very presence threatened his trade. But what of the others? Walter, Anna and Old Harold? Zeb, Rose-Marie, Rick and Adam . . . Surely these people were not involved?

'Has your father gone yet?'

She nodded.

'When?'

'About fifteen minutes ago. That was the first time I had a chance to slip out. I came down here as soon as the coast was clear. I had to see if you were OK, Piggy. It's all my fault.'

'I have to warn them,' said Ben. 'I have to get back out there and warn them before it's too late.'

He pushed himself away from the support of the barn door.

'We could go together,' she said. 'You're still weak. It'd take you ages to get there. We could saddle up Champion. Dad and the others have gone in four-wheel drives. They have to go round by one of the old quarry roads to get into the heart of the woods. That's what they said. If we head along Foxglove Ride we'll have a head start.

You can give me directions after that. I want to help.'

Ben took her hand and they crossed the small yard.

He was weaker than he had thought. He leaned on the stable wall while Rachel went in and prepared her pony. His head was spinning, his heart racing.

'Come in here, Piggy,' she said after a few long minutes.

He pushed himself upright and walked slowly inside.

Rachel was sitting in the saddle already. 'Come on,' she said. 'There's a mounting block we use for children when they come for riding lessons. Just over here. Come on. Climb up.' She leaned over and took his hand. 'That's it. Now hold on to me and swing your leg over.'

He took a deep breath and lifted his leg. She caught his foot and guided it over, and he slid into the small space in the saddle behind her.

'Hold on,' she said.

He wrapped his arms around her and rested his head on her back.

They headed out into the darkness at a slow walk. He had to concentrate. He had to keep his balance and not give in to the dizziness that threatened to overcome him. He felt close to fainting.

They headed along the track towards Weeley Woods.

Smugglers

He heard the call. An animal sound, but made by no animal. It was the lookouts' alarm cry, a warning that there were vampires near the community.

For a moment, Ben thought they must be too late, that Rachel's father had beaten them there. But no; there were no gunshots, no sounds of engines, or other disturbance. Just the warning call. And then he realized; they had spotted him and Rachel. That was why the alarm was being raised.

The alarm changed to an insistent, double note.

Ben could imagine the well-rehearsed drill; the ferals following secret routes into the woods where they would hide until the danger had passed. But he knew the danger would not pass on this night. This was only the beginning.

'Are you sure?' Rachel said yet again. The track through a thick barrier of bramble appeared to be coming to a dead end, but Ben knew that this was a clever illusion. Only when you reached the end would you see a small opening, a gap you could pass through.

'Keep going,' he said. 'The way to the community is disguised.'

She dismounted, leaving Ben to cling uncertainly to the saddle as she led Champion on through the narrow path.

When they emerged in the clearing there was nothing to be seen. It was a moonlit night, but the dark shapes of the shelters were lost in the heaped brambles and ivy that had been grown to disguise them. There was no sign of movement. No sign that anyone had ever lived there.

Ben slid from the saddle and Rachel just managed to catch him as he staggered on landing.

'Walter,' he called. 'Walter. It's me, Ben. Please come back, Walter. They're coming. I have to warn you; they're coming!'

He was talking to an empty clearing. Wasting his time. They were probably out of earshot already.

And then there was movement. A figure appeared from the trees. Walter. He was followed by two more: the brothers, Rick and Adam.

Walter approached Ben and Rachel, and the boys hung back a short distance.

'What's going on?' Walter demanded in a low voice. 'What have you brought one of them here for?'

'I had to warn you,' said Ben. He felt dizzy again. Exhausted by the ride. 'I was caught. They drank my blood. They know about this place. They know what Alik's been doing. They're coming . . . I had to warn you . . . I had to . . .'

He hit the ground with a thud.

When he came round Walter was shaking him gently.

'It's true,' Ben heard Rachel saying. 'They're coming here. The local families. Coming along the old quarry road.'

'The quarry?' said Walter urgently. 'You're sure about that?'

199

Ben sat up and saw Rachel nodding.

Walter turned to the two brothers. 'Rick, Adam,' he said. 'You get out there and warn the others, OK? Get them out of there.'

'What's going on?' said Ben. 'What's so special about the quarry?'

'Zeb's there,' said Walter. 'And some of the others. That's where they meet the trading families. The beasts.' He almost spat the word out, staring at Rachel.

'Do you know what they trade?' asked Ben steadily.

Walter looked at him curiously. 'Anything and everything,' he said. 'Anything we forage that we can't use in the woods.'

'They trade people,' said Ben softly. 'My story was true. I'm not from this world. People from my world – probably from other worlds too – are smuggled here and traded with the beasts. People for protection, that's the deal.'

Walter shook his head. 'That's not true,' he said. 'I don't believe you.'

'It started about three or four years ago,' said Rachel. 'New varieties of wild blood, put on the market by families that didn't even keep ... didn't have piggeries.'

Walter's expression had changed. 'Alik was seriously ill about five years ago,' he said. 'Fevers, delirium. He was hallucinating. Hallucinating about other worlds. He's never been the same since.'

'Old Harold says that some people are sensitive to the places where worlds come close together,' said Ben. The passageways must have existed for a long time – Old Harold was evidence of that – but the traders had only been using them in recent years. 'Alik must be sensitive. Maybe it was triggered by his illness. Or maybe his illness was triggered by the worlds somehow coming closer together ...'

'You think he can control this thing? You think he can open up passages between worlds?'

'Either that or he can sense when breaches are about to open up and he's learned how to exploit them.'

'Madness,' said Walter. 'It's all madness.'

But Ben could see doubt in the man's eyes.

*

Ben insisted on going with them. Walter helped him up on to Champion's back and then he and Rachel led the pony along a well-used trail that led to the old quarry.

Soon they could hear people up ahead. Ben recognized the voices of Rick and Adam, and Robby, shouting at them. Others too.

The trees retreated from either side of the path and they emerged on a track that cut down across one of the faces of the old workings. There were people down there, arguing. And one man, standing apart, oblivious to the disturbance.

It was Alik, standing with his arms spread, his head bowed. He was facing the cliff-wall and then Ben saw what was taking up his attention.

The rocky wall flickered and shimmered, as if Ben was looking at it through a heat haze.

It was there, but it *wasn't* there. It was somewhere else. Some world else. An opening between worlds . . . just as Old Harold had said. Old Harold, who so long ago had given up believing that it could be true . . .

'That's it,' Ben gasped. 'That's the way through.' But through to where?

Walter had left them. He had seen Zeb and had marched across and seized the tall young man's arm. 'Even you!' he cried. 'Even you, my own son, are involved in this!'

Zeb tried to shake free of his father's grip, but he couldn't. 'It's survival,' he said. 'Just like you always taught me. Sometimes we have to do things we don't like, just to survive. That's all we've been doing.'

Ben slid down from the horse. He went across to Walter and Zeb. 'You knew all along, didn't you?' he said to Zeb. His voice was low and weak, but it seemed to cut through the chaos. 'You knew my story was true – that's why you stuck with me. You weren't trying to help me. You were trying to see how much I knew about what was going on!'

Zeb wouldn't meet his look. 'It wasn't like that,' he said. 'You must have come through by chance. I didn't know for sure. And then we found you and talked to you and . . . you're just like us!'

Ben felt sickened: When they traded people they must have somehow blinded themselves to the fact that it was people they were rustling, and not just 'livestock'.

'You don't think I felt guilty?' asked Zeb.

'But did it stop you?' Ben cried.

'We have to carry on,' said Zeb. 'We need the protection.'

'You're just the same as them,' said Ben. 'Just as bad as Rachel's father.'

'All this time!' murmured Walter. 'All this time you knew that there was another world, a *safe* world, and you kept it secret!'

Then Robby butted in. 'Sure,' he said. 'There are other worlds – some far worse than this! You think they wouldn't hunt us down there? You think we could just settle in unnoticed? We don't belong there. At least we've had protection here. At least the trade has bought us protection, old man. If it wasn't for the likes of us, the community would have been wiped out years ago!'

'Are you sure about that?' asked Walter. 'Are you really sure that there was no alternative?'

For a moment there was silence, as if everyone was letting this sink in. Ben looked around. A lot of the woodlanders were there – they had either been there already with Alik or they had followed Walter and Ben. It was as if they had all felt the need to stay close together tonight.

And now they were all in danger.

There was a roar of engines from the road, the crunch of tyres on the loose, stony surface.

'They're coming!' called Ben. 'Can't you hear? They're coming.'

He turned to the shimmering rock wall. Alik seemed oblivious to what was going on around him. Whatever he was doing – holding the passageway open or simply responding to its presence – seemed to be taking up all his concentration.

Ben stared at the flickering, distorting surface. Where did it lead to? He looked at Alik. 'You can see through, can't you? You can see into the next world.'

Just for an instant, his words seemed to get through to the man. 'The worlds are close,' he gasped. 'Yours . . . mine . . . but not for long . . .'

Alik was offering them the chance to escape. But what about the piggeries? What about the woodlanders who weren't there in the quarry? Old Harold was probably still in his treehouse – what about him?

They had to act, and they had to do it now. They had this chance and it might be their only one.

Ben turned to Rachel. 'Thank you,' he said. 'I won't forget what you've done for me.'

She shrugged. 'I got half the blood sucked from your body, didn't I? I got you locked up with all the other piggies. Sure,' she said. 'You'll remember me all right.'

He stepped forward and hugged her. 'I don't mean that,' he said. 'I'll remember the good things.'

He released her and turned towards the passageway. 'Come on,' he called to the others. 'This is our only chance.'

Close to, he could feel the intense energy of the opening. He looked back. They didn't have long. The others were staring at him. They had stopped arguing and fighting. They were scared.

'Come on,' said Ben. He waved a hand towards the quarry entrance. 'They're coming.'

Five or six big cars had stopped at the chained-up gate. Figures had emerged, picked out by the vehicles' headlights. Already, they were scrambling over the gate. Ben saw a sudden glint of dark metal. They were carrying guns.

'Come on!'

And then another voice said, 'Go on! Do as he says!' It was Alik. He was shaking, tears running down his face.

They took no more persuading. First Walter, then Zeb and the others approached Ben. One by one, they stepped into the shimmering rock face and vanished. Ben was the last to go.

'Go,' hissed Alik. 'Tell them I'm sorry. Tell them I was only trying to protect them.'

The beasts were almost upon him.

Ben stepped through the rock face.

Suddenly, the air was sucked from his lungs and he felt powerful forces tugging at his limbs. He twisted and turned, fighting the pressure. He felt as if he was in mid-air, spinning.

He cried out . . .

. . . and landed in a heap on the ground.

He was confused, muddled, his head spinning.

Everywhere was wet and he'd landed in the mud. It was raining.

He rolled over, lay back, let the rain soak him through. It felt good.

He was home. At last, he had made it back to his own world.

Home Again

It took them a while to gather themselves.

'It's a bit hit and miss,' Zeb explained. 'The opening's not predictable – there's a central focus, the main passageway, but there are other openings too, spread out. That must be how you stumbled through,' he told Ben '– wrong place at the wrong time.'

'You sound well practised in these things,' said Walter, still angry.

Zeb looked away. 'We were trying to buy protection, that's all.'

Eventually, they found everyone who had made it through the passageway. A good proportion of the woodlanders had made the journey between worlds. What would happen to those left behind? Ben hoped they would be able to hide themselves until the families' anger had died down. Maybe another rift would open up and they would be able to escape. Maybe Alik would help them, if he managed to evade the beasts.

The people farmed in the piggeries wouldn't have that chance, though. They would continue their short lives of suffering. If only he could have done something! But no . . . What more could he have done on his own? At least the 'livestock' smuggling was at an end and he had helped this group of woodlanders to escape.

'What will you do?' asked Ben. How would they survive in a world they didn't know?

'We'll get by,' said Walter. 'We've found somewhere new and, in any case, we're used to survival.'

'I'll do what I can,' said Ben. 'I'll help you learn how things work here. What you have to look out for. You're in a better place.'

Walter shook his head. 'Ben,' he said. 'This is your world. What must your family be thinking? You need to go back to them and show them you're OK. We'll be all right, Ben. Just think of us if you ever hear stories of a group of strange travellers who don't quite fit in, OK?'

For some time, he watched out for any reports in the news, but there was nothing. There were so many strange people who didn't quite fit into the world though. How do you tell one peculiar story from another?

Ben was in the news himself, for a time – a boy who had gone missing and then returned again three weeks later. He wanted to tell someone, but it was hard to find the words. Words that would not sound stupid, words that would convince grown-ups that there was so much more to reality than they had ever imagined.

It was easier, at first, to pretend not to remember. He told his parents and the police that all he could recall was blacking out on his way home from Andy's, and then waking up again in the middle of the woods, wandering aimlessly, lost and confused. He didn't know what had happened in-between those times. At least, he couldn't tell them anything they'd believe.

211

Some days after his return, he tried to tell Andy. He was the one person who might take his claims seriously. Andy listened without interrupting, and when Ben had finished his friend just sat there with that dopey grin on his face.

'So,' he said, at last. 'Let's get this straight. Another world. Vampires. People farmed like pigs. You've been reading those books again, haven't you?'

Angrily, Ben said, 'OK, I can prove it.' He pulled at the collar of his football shirt, tugged it down to reveal his neck. 'Look,' he said. 'See where McDonnell bit me.'

Andy leaned forward, then sat back, shaking his head. 'Nothing there,' he said.

Ben put a finger to his neck and felt smooth skin. The marks had been there that morning. He was sure. But now they had gone. Healed.

He slumped back on the sofa, questioning his own sanity. But then he remembered Rachel's words: *You're the one who's been through it, whatever it is. You need to trust your own judgement, Piggy.*

'Listen,' said Andy. 'You sure had me going

for a few minutes though. You and your stories . . .'

It was hard to settle back into normal life. He couldn't pass the town's medical practice without horrible flashbacks to the other world, to the policeman and the doctor whose baby sucked blood from its mother's neck.

The strangest things brought up disturbing memories, which threatened to swamp him. In the supermarket with his parents, the press of bodies, the mindless noise . . . and suddenly he was back in the piggery, surrounded by snuffling and grunting and jostling, naked bodies.

But they were just tricks, played by his mind. He was safe now. He was back in his own world and all that was behind him.

Or so he thought.

He spotted her in the high street. It was only the second time he'd been allowed out on his own since his return.

She was wandering along, just staring. Looking all around in wonderment. The spiky blonde hair, the tight jeans and the baggy black jumper she had been wearing that night. He shook himself. This couldn't be happening. It was just someone who looked like Rachel. Or it was some kind of flashback, some kind of illusion. It wasn't happening.

But it was.

She saw him, she smiled, she came to join him, standing by the spitting fish fountain.

'Piggy,' she said, in a small, nervous voice.

She looked scared, lost.

'I followed you through,' she said. 'In all the confusion, I followed you through. I've been here ever since. I didn't really believe you, Piggy. No matter how hard I tried, I didn't believe you.

'But it's true, Piggy. It really is true – a whole world like this!'

He had been mistaken. At first he had thought she was scared; terrified to find herself in a strange new world. But no. That wasn't fear in her eyes. It was something else.

Rachel was excited.

And Rachel was hungry . . .

www.puffin.co.uk.www.puffin.co.uk.www.puffin.co.uk
bookinfo.competitions.news.games.sneakpreviews
www.puffin.co.uk.www.puffin.co.uk.www.puffin.co.uk
adventure.bestsellers.fun.coollinks.freestuff
www.puffin.co.uk.www.puffin.co.uk.www.puffin.co.uk
explore.yourshout.awards.toptips.authorinfo
www.puffin.co.uk.www.puffin.co.uk.www.puffin.co.uk
greatbooks.greatbooks.greatbooks.greatbooks
www.puffin.co.uk.www.puffin.co.uk.www.puffin.co.uk
reviews.poems.jokes.authorevents.audioclips
www.puffin.co.uk.www.puffin.co.uk.www.puffin.co.uk
interviews.e-mailupdates.bookinfo.competitions.news

www.puffin.co.uk

games.sneakpreviews.adventure.bestsellers.fun
www.puffin.co.uk.www.puffin.co.uk.www.puffin.co.uk
bookinfo.competitions.news.games.sneakpreviews
www.puffin.co.uk.www.puffin.co.uk.www.puffin.co.uk
adventure.bestsellers.fun.coollinks.freestuff
www.puffin.co.uk.www.puffin.co.uk.www.puffin.co.uk
explore.yourshout.awards.toptips.authorinfo
www.puffin.co.uk.www.puffin.co.uk.www.puffin.co.uk
greatbooks.greatbooks.greatbooks.greatbooks
www.puffin.co.uk.www.puffin.co.uk.www.puffin.co.uk
reviews.poems.jokes.authorevents.audioclips
www.puffin.co.uk.www.puffin.co.uk.www.puffin.co.uk

www.puffin.co.uk.www.puffin.co.uk.www.puffin.co.uk

bookinfo.competitions.news.games.sneakpreviews

www.puffin.co.uk.www.puffin.co.uk.www.puffin.co.uk

adventure.bestsellers.fun.coollinks.freestuff

www.puffin.co.uk.www.puffin.co.uk.www.puffin.co.uk

explore.yourshout.awards.toptips.authorinfo

www.puffin.co.uk.www.puffin.co.uk.www.puffin.co.uk

greatbooks.greatbooks.greatbooks.greatbooks

www.puffin.co.uk.www.puffin.co.uk.www.puffin.co.uk

reviews.poems.jokes.authorevents.audioclips

www.puffin.co.uk.www.puffin.co.uk.www.puffin.co.uk

interviews.e-mailupdates.bookinfo.competitions.news

www.puffin.co.uk

games.sneakpreviews.adventure.bestsellers.fun

www.puffin.co.uk.www.puffin.co.uk.www.puffin.co.uk

bookinfo.competitions.news.games.sneakpreviews

www.puffin.co.uk.www.puffin.co.uk.www.puffin.co.uk

adventure.bestsellers.fun.coollinks.freestuff

www.puffin.co.uk.www.puffin.co.uk.www.puffin.co.uk

explore.yourshout.awards.toptips.authorinfo

www.puffin.co.uk.www.puffin.co.uk.www.puffin.co.uk

greatbooks.greatbooks.greatbooks.greatbooks

www.puffin.co.uk.www.puffin.co.uk.www.puffin.co.uk

reviews.poems.jokes.authorevents.audioclips

www.puffin.co.uk.www.puffin.co.uk.www.puffin.co.uk